POISONED IN PORT TOWNSEND

A PACIFIC NORTHWEST COZY CULINARY MYSTERY SERIES - BOOK 2

DENNIS SHOCK

1

Lily's phone rang, and she glanced at it for a split second. It was Detective Doug Miller. She didn't have time to talk since the lunch rush at the restaurant had already started. She would have to call him back after business slowed down. She slid the cell phone into her apron pocket. Lily was busy on expo, setting up trays of food to be taken to tables in the dining room. She liked to be the last check on food quality as it left the window. She spent most lunch hours running the window. She never let subpar plates leave her kitchen. She enjoyed the hustle and bustle of the kitchen and the feeling of accomplishment as the trays of food were carried out into the dining room.

Lily would try to remember to call Doug back later. Her kitchen manager, Linda Holt, would be in to help with the main lunch rush and work the dinner hour. Chase Raker would be in at night to oversee the dining room and close the place down after dinner. For the first few months her restaurant, Marty's on the Bay, was open, Lily worked open to close with no time for herself. By the time her Poulsbo restaurant reached its ninth month, she had learned to trust in her management team and had since begun to take some free time for herself.

Lily Pine's daughter, Judy, sat at the large mahogany bar with her laptop out, nursing a tall glass of iced tea. She was an investigative reporter for *The Seattle Times*. She moved to the Kitsap Peninsula from Ohio several months ago to be near her mother. Judy lived in the nearby town of Silverdale but spent much of her time at her mother's restaurant, as she could work from anywhere. She traveled the Kitsap Peninsula, in person and on the Internet, in search of news stories. She often did her actual writing from the bar stool where she was currently sitting. In addition to being a great investigative reporter, she was an incredible online researcher.

When the lunch rush ended, the restaurant started to empty out. "Are you working or playing on the Internet?" Lily asked her daughter as she pulled out the stool next to her.

"I'm looking at dogs." She grinned.

"Are you thinking about getting a dog? I think that's a marvelous idea."

"You should get a little dog. I'm sure Nellie would enjoy the company." Nellie was a short and stout Petit Basset Griffon Vendéen that Lily had adopted in Ohio almost ten years ago. Nellie was a sweet soul who loved people and other dogs, for the most part. "She takes walks with

Brick most weekends, but I'm sure she would enjoy having another companion of her same species."

"I know Jed brings Brick by on Sundays, but Jed rarely has time during the week and that big lug of a Goldendoodle has to be a little intimidating for Nellie to be around. Admittedly, a puppy would likely drive her crazy at first, but I'm sure they'll work it out in time and grow to be great friends. A lady in Port Townsend works with a Yorkshire Terrier rescue group. Do you want to go with me to see the puppies they are currently trying to place in good homes?" Judy turned the laptop screen towards her mother. Three tiny, furry, black faces with wide brown eyes looked through the screen at Lily.

Lily couldn't help but smile at the faces of the adorable pups. "Nellie gets along quite well with Brick, but I think Yorkies are adorable. I'd love to go along if you can do it when I have time. I would like to check in with Mrs. Carver while we are there. She picked up a large box lunch order yesterday. She's a great customer, and I always like to check back after her events to make sure everyone enjoyed the food. It would be great to check in with her in person."

"Two birds. Can you go this afternoon?"

Before Lily could answer her daughter, Sharon Robbins rushed through the restaurant's front entrance towards Lily and Judy. Sharon was a tall, strong woman in her thirties. She moved with purpose through the dining room.

"Did you hear about Doug?" Sharon asked, looking at Lily.

"Oh, he tried to call me earlier. I haven't called him back yet."

"He's been in a terrible car accident," Sharon continued. "He's in the hospital."

2

"Doug. I'm sorry I didn't take your call," Lily wanted to hear his voice. She wanted to hear him say he was okay. "Sharon told me about your accident. If I had some way to know you were hurt..."

"It's okay. Thanks for calling me back. I know it's hard for you to take a call over the lunch hour. First of all, I'm okay. Don't worry. I actually tried to call you before the accident. I was assigned to a case in Port Townsend that involves you."

"I'm very happy to hear that you are all right. What kind of case? How does one of your cases involve me?"

"A widower who lived in Port Townsend was found dead yesterday. He was in his late seventies. There was no reason to believe his death might be a homicide until the coroner completed the autopsy. The lab report showed sodium cyanide in his system."

"What does that have to do with me?"

"He died in his kitchen near a mostly eaten cookie. Crime scene investigators bagged a box lunch at the scene.

The cookie from the box also tested positive for cyanide. The box came from Marty's on the Bay. The evidence points back to your restaurant."

"Oh, my. I don't know what to say. Of course, you know that the poison didn't come from my restaurant."

"I know you didn't poison the cookie. I don't know that someone didn't poison the cookie before it left the restaurant. I was on point to contact you and see about getting into your place for some tests. Lily, I need you to pull all the cookies for testing. We will need to get forensics into your restaurant to rule out any traces of cyanide there."

"I'll have to close for dinner. Out of an abundance of caution, I need to make sure there hasn't been some kind of contamination here on the premises. Everything has slowed down from the lunch rush. We'll stop letting people in the restaurant. I'll close the place down immediately. Hold on a minute."

Lily put the phone on hold as she approached Chase and Linda in the dining room. "Hey, you two. Put the closed sign up. Don't let anyone else in. Let the staff know that we will be closed for dinner tonight. No one eats anything here the rest of the day." The two managers stood before Lily with their eyes wide and their jaws open. "Go on. Do as I said. I'll explain shortly."

Lily clicked the hold button on her phone and walked back to the office. "Are you sure you're okay? What happened?"

"A truck driver lost control of his rig on the Narrows Bridge. My car is totaled. I have a few broken bones but nothing that won't heal. Don't worry about me. Local PD will be there soon with a court order. Jim Handler will be taking over the poison case since I'm out of commission. He's not the sharpest tool in the shed, but he will get the lab guys on this. Hopefully, they'll confirm everything is fine in the restaurant, and you can get back to business while we figure this thing out."

"Okay. We are closing down. Hopefully, just for the day. I'll be down to see you once the police are finished."

"That's not necessary, Lil. I'm fine. I should be out of here in a day or two."

"We were already planning to go to Port Townsend tonight to check on a customer and a puppy. We'll come to see you first before we go to Port Townsend. If it gets too late, we can go there tomorrow. Can I bring you anything?"

"A puppy? Did you say you were going to check on a puppy?"

"I did. Not for me. For Judy. She is considering it."

"I wouldn't say no to some soup. Something about soup always makes me feel better. No matter the ailment."

"I'll be happy to deliver some soup to you. We'll pick some up on the way. You wouldn't want anything from the restaurant right now. Would you like a sandwich or maybe some dessert? I'm happy to bring you whatever you would like."

"Just some soup would be great."

"You got it. Judy and I will be down as soon as we can."

"Oh, good. I haven't seen Judy in a while. How's she doing? How's the new job?"

"She seems very happy here. She likes the area and the people at the paper. I'm sure she will be happy to tell you all about it."

"She's never bashful, that's for sure," Doug said with a soft chuckle.

Lily was happy to hear him laugh. She was starting to believe he really was okay. Lily and Doug had a bit of an emotional connection after becoming acquainted during a murder investigation. They had shared several meals together and had some open conversations over the past several months. Lily valued their friendship and thought Doug did as well. Though it started as a bit of a romance, they had settled into more of a sibling-type relationship.

"I should go. Officer Treadwell is here." Lily could see the officer through her office window.

"Good to hear. I like him. He's a fine young officer. Let me know how it goes."

3

"You look pretty banged up. Are you sure you're okay?" Lily winced a bit as she approached Doug Miller's hospital bed.

"Yeah. Holy crap, Doug. You look like you got hit by a truck." Judy grinned from behind Lily.

"Yep. This is what it looks like. I'm doing okay. I'm glad it didn't take the forensics team all night to collect evidence."

"I don't know if I'd call it evidence exactly," Lily protested softly.

"Everything involved is evidence," Judy injected. "They collect evidence to rule things out as well as determine fault. Hopefully, it won't take them long to rule the restaurant out. Then, we will need to figure out how the poison ended up in one of your cookies. If a story goes public that someone was poisoned with one of your cookies... well, it could ruin the restaurant," Judy said shaking her head.

"Hopefully, it won't come to that, Judy. They tested Mr. Creech's blood right away since he was sitting at the table with food in front of him when he died. Cyanide only stays in the system for a couple of days, so they had to check for poisons fairly quickly. We should have lab results on the food back tomorrow. Hopefully, that will put the restaurant in the clear, and then we will look further into the case before letting the media have any details. My understanding is that the cookie was mostly eaten, but the rest of the lunch was untouched. Hopefully, we can count on Detective Handler to keep the source of the food under wraps while the investigation moves forward. Ruling out the restaurant for having any trace of cyanide is important, but the best-case scenario is that they find that the poison didn't come from your restaurant at all. Lily, did you meet Detective Handler?"

"I did. He came in while the lab guys were there. Not the sweetest man I've met on the peninsula."

"Don't sugarcoat it, Mom. He was rude and condescending. He has a high opinion of himself. He told Mom she couldn't reopen until he told her she could. Does he make that decision?"

"The evidence will make the decision, but he will be the one to let you know when and if you can reopen. If there's any problem, I'll get my superiors involved. You may not get to open for lunch tomorrow. Keep that in mind."

"But we could possibly open tomorrow?" Lily was trying to stay positive.

"I have been on the phone with everyone I know at the lab. They are trying to get tests run as quickly as possible on all the samples from your place. Initial tests just need to come back negative for cyanide. That should get you open."

"Either way, I think cookies are off the menu until this whole thing is over." Lily sighed deeply. "What's the extent of your injuries here? Can we take you home soon?"

"My leg is in pretty bad shape. The orthopedic surgeon is going to have to do some work on me tomorrow. Most of the rest are just scratches and bruises. I'll need a ride home eventually. My car is toast. I'm off-duty until I recover, which will give me time to look for a new vehicle. Don't worry, I'll stay abreast of your case."

"Detective Handler asked me and my staff about Mr. Creech. No one had ever heard of him except for David. He's one of my cooks," Lily informed him.

"How does he know Norman Creech?" Doug asked.

"He grew up in Port Townsend. I think Mr. Creech was a friend of the family," Lily responded.

"He didn't say it to Handler, but David told me Norman Creech wasn't a very well-liked man. David used to live and work in Port Townsend at a restaurant on their main shopping strip. He said Mr. Creech would come in and grumble about everything and leave without tipping the staff. He was known to be a wealthy man but was also a tightwad. According to what I could look up on my way here, the deceased owned several rental properties around Port Townsend. He made a ton of his money renting out bungalows along the water. They look like the kind of places you would rent for a short period to sit by the water or kayak from the shoreline." Judy shared what she had learned.

"How did the box lunch end up in his house? Do you know if he was in your restaurant today or yesterday?" Doug looked from Judy to Lily.

"Detective Handler asked me the same question. No one on my staff remembered him being in the restaurant at all. We checked credit card receipts for the past month without turning up his name. The only thing that makes any sense is that he may have gotten the meal from a customer of mine in Port Townsend who picked up forty box lunches yesterday morning. It was for a charity luncheon. I don't know how Norman Creech would have ended up with one if he wasn't a charitable man, but I don't have a better hypothesis," Lily said.

"I bet one of the attendees poisoned the cookie and then gave the box lunch to the crotchety Mr. Creech. Being the cheapskate that he is, he was more than happy to get a free lunch. It's a working theory. I don't have any proof, but I intend to follow up on it. No one else was poisoned, right?" Judy was eager to get involved in the case.

"No other reports of poisoning. You two should leave this up to the lead investigator. Don't go poking around where there may be a killer. Whoever poisoned this man is dangerous." Doug winced in pain as he shifted his weight as much as possible in the bed.

"You already said Detective Handler wasn't very smart. If we wait for him to figure this thing out, Mom could be out of business before she gets to Marty on the Bay's one-year anniversary," Judy scoffed.

"I shouldn't have made that comment about Jim. I'm sure he'll get this all resolved in no time." Doug waited for confirmation that the ladies believed his comment but received no such reaction.

"We should let you get some rest." Lily placed her hand on Doug's shoulder for a moment. "Oh, I almost forgot. I have tortilla soup, corn chips, and grated cheese for you. I'll ask at the desk to see if someone can warm it up for you." Lily pulled a plastic container from her large handbag.

"I'll take care of that," Judy said as she took the sealed container from her mother and exited the room.

"Please don't put yourself in any danger," Doug paused for confirmation, "again."

"We'll be careful, but we need to look into this. That restaurant was my husband's dream. It means a lot to me. We will just try to gather information on how the cookie came to be in the presence of Mr. Creech. You know how Judy is. Her investigative reporter hat will be on the second we leave here. She wants to help me and, of course, sees a story in this for the paper. I had already planned to follow up with the Port Townsend customer before we heard about the poisoning. Mrs. Carver may know how the box lunch ended up in Mr. Creech's possession. Since there are no other reports of illness or death it sounds like only one lunch was contaminated."

"The cookie was the only item from the box that had been opened. It appeared that the rest of the lunch was untouched. It seems that sour Mr. Creech had a sweet tooth."

"I imagine the entire lunch is at the lab now being tested. Will you please let me know when you get any results from the lab? I need to know if any of this is truly related to my restaurant. I won't reopen until we can be sure my food is safe to eat."

"I understand. We will get news to you that is pertinent to your business. That will not be overstepping on my part. That's a need-to-know kind of thing."

"Thank you."

Judy re-entered the hospital room holding the container of soup with several napkins. "It's hot now," she said as she pulled the rolling tray table up to Doug, handing him a spoon.

Doug opened the plastic container and took a deep whiff of the soup. "It smells delicious. Thank you for bringing this. I'm sure it will be much more appetizing than the hospital food."

"We stopped at that specialty market that prepares fresh, ready-to-eat meals," Lily said.

"Oh, that's sweet of you. You didn't need to go to such trouble," Doug said as he brought the first spoonful to his lips.

"No trouble at all." Lily smiled at him.

"It's delicious." Doug continued to eat the steaming, hot soup. "What about the puppy? Did you get a puppy?" He looked at Judy.

"We decided it would be late by the time we got there tonight. I had to reschedule the visit." Judy frowned.

"The forensics team took longer than expected at the restaurant, and then you were our priority," Lily said with a smile.

"I'm honored," he grinned.

4

J udy knocked at the door of Mrs. Carver's office in downtown Port Townsend. Lily stood next to Judy with nervous anticipation as the door opened swiftly.

"Hi, Lily. Is this your daughter I've heard so much about?" Martha Carver, a tall, nicely dressed, sandy-haired woman in her fifties, extended her hand to each of her visitors and then moved behind her desk. "Please, have a seat."

"Yes, this is Judy. We wanted to stop by to check on how your catering order was received."

"Splendid. The sandwiches and cookies were delightful, as always. That broccoli salad was a nice touch. Thank you for recommending that. I called most of the philanthropists who attended to check in with them after I heard about Mr. Creech. Detective Handler asked me to check with everyone who ate one of the box lunches. I was able to get ahold of all but two of them," Martha offered.

"Was Mr. Creech at your meeting?" Judy asked.

"No. Mr. Creech isn't much for philanthropy. He was a wealthy man but did not make a habit of sharing his wealth."

"How did he get one of my mom's box lunches?"

"His nephew is on the board for one of my charities. Jeff Donavan is very charity-minded but sadly not as wealthy as his uncle. We had box lunches left over after the meeting. He asked if he could take one for his uncle. I'm not sure but Jeff may be Norman Creech's only living relative. He tried to take care of his uncle. Norman Creech was not in the best of health," Mrs. Carver shook her head as she spoke.

"The nephew was at the meeting and left here with a box lunch that presumably ended up killing Mr. Creech. No one else who ate the lunches fell ill that you know of?" Lily was summarizing what they had learned from Mrs. Carver.

"The detective asked about the health of everyone who attended the luncheon, so I spoke to almost everyone after he questioned me. He asked specifically about the cookies. Everyone I talked to said they ate the cookies and loved them. They did not report feeling ill in the slightest. I'm not sure what happened to Norman, but I doubt it was the fault of your restaurant. I don't see how it could have been. I gave Detective Handler a copy of the guest list. He will likely be following up with everyone as well." Martha seemed to be stewing on her words.

"So, either just the one lunch was contaminated before it arrived here, or it became contaminated between here and Norman Creech's kitchen table. Can you tell us how we might be able to get in touch with Jeff Donavan?" Judy asked.

"Oh, yes. His office is a block from here. He's an accountant. He works out of an office at the corner of Fifth and Main. He might not be there considering what happened to his uncle, but they will know how to reach him."

"Thank you. That's very helpful." Judy's wheels were spinning. She was anxious to follow up with Norman's nephew to try to prove her mother's restaurant had nothing to do with his uncle's death.

"I'm happy to hear that everyone else is okay. Thank you for your time." Lily stood and reached for Martha's hand. Her daughter followed suit, and the two women left the office.

As they exited the building on Main Street, Judy turned immediately towards Fifth. "Let's go see Jeff Donavan. We need to know where that box lunch was every second from the time it left here with him until he served it to his uncle. Chances are someone contaminated it before it arrived at Mr. Creech's home."

"I understand we need to prove that the food from my restaurant didn't cause Mr. Creech's death, but either way it is disturbing to think someone may have used one of my cookies as a weapon to kill a person."

5

J udy marched through the door of the small accounting office on the corner. Lily followed closely behind her. Judy smiled at the elderly lady at the desk and started with an introduction. "Hi. I'm Judy Pine, and this is Lily. We are here to see Mr. Donavan. Is he in?"

The small-framed woman behind the desk looked over her reading glasses at Judy. "Mr. Donavan is with someone at the moment. Do you ladies have an appointment?"

"No, we don't. We were hoping to talk to Mr. Donavan about his uncle," Lily said from behind her daughter.

"Mr. Donavan is with a detective discussing that very thing," the receptionist whispered. "There's no telling what might have happened to old Mr. Creech. Mr. Donavan is only related to the man by marriage, but Jeff was the only relative Norman Creech had left in town; heaven knows the old coot didn't have any friends."

"We are wondering if you saw Mr. Donavan with a box lunch the day Norman Creech died. It would have been a box about this big." Judy raised her hands and positioned them about a foot apart and then moved them to show a height of about four inches.

"It would have been purple with a bright yellow smiley face on it," Lily added.

"Oh, yes. He came in with that box around noon. It was after his meeting with the charity organization down the street. I remember because he sat it down on the corner of my desk, and I told him I had already eaten. He made a joke about it not being for me anyway." The receptionist tapped the top of her desk closest to the door.

"Did he leave it there for long?" Judy asked.

"He wasn't here for more than twenty or thirty minutes. I'm not sure exactly. I went in the back to file some papers, and when I got back, Mr. Donavan and the box were both gone."

A voice came over an intercom system behind the desk, "Mrs. Brown. Can you come in here, please?"

The elderly receptionist tapped a button on her phone and said, "Yes, Mr. Donavan." She got up from behind her desk and whispered to Judy and Lily again, "I'll let him know you're here. You can have a seat by the door if you like." She turned and walked towards the back of the building.

"Detective Handler likely just found out from Jeff Donavan that the lunch box was left on Mrs. Brown's desk. I bet they called her back there to question her. She didn't have anything nice to say about Mr. Creech," Judy whispered to her mother as she tapped the corner of the desk where the receptionist had said the box was placed.

"Come now. You don't believe that nice, little, old lady killed Mr. Creech, do you?"

"Hard to say. We don't know any of these people or what they are capable of." Judy continued to keep her voice low. "Jeff may have poisoned the cookie. Mrs. Brown could have done it … or anyone in this office for that matter. Jeff Donavan left the box with Mrs. Brown, who left it sitting here while she went to the file room. Any number of people had access to it."

"But did any number of people know who was going to eat it?"

"Maybe the culprit didn't care whom he killed. Maybe it was a random act. There are a lot of crazy people in the world."

Mrs. Brown shuffled back to her desk with her reading glasses swinging from a chain around her neck. "Mr. Donavan and Detective Handler will see you now. Last door on the right." She pointed in the direction she had just come from.

Judy shrugged and walked briskly down the hall. Lily followed closely behind her daughter, thanking the grey-haired receptionist as she passed. The last door on the right was open. Judy stepped into the room. As Lily came into their view, the two men standing in the middle of the room smiled. "Mrs. Pine. It's nice to see you again," the detective said. "This is Mrs. Pine from the restaurant the box lunch came from. I believe this is her daughter with her."

"I'm Judy Pine. We stopped by to offer our condolences." Judy nodded softly in Jeff's direction. "You are Jeff Donavan, aren't you?"

"Yes, ma'am. I'm Mr. Creech's nephew. Thank you."

"We were very sorry to hear about your uncle." Lily stepped forward and offered her hand to Jeff.

"That's very kind of you. Did you know my uncle?" he asked as he shook her hand gently.

"No. I didn't. I am devastated that my food could have had something to do with this awful tragedy and ... well... I'm very sorry to hear about your uncle."

"Do you know for sure that the food from the box lunch is what killed him? Are you sure it was the cookie?" Judy shifted her gaze to Detective Handler.

"Cyanide works pretty quickly. He had a good amount in his system based on the results of the autopsy. We are testing the cookie among other items in the house now, but the forensic team is fairly certain that the cookie contained cyanide." Detective Handler pulled some eight-by-eleven photos from a folder he had in his hand. "Do you recognize this box, Lily?" He turned the photo towards the two ladies.

"Yes, that's one of my box lunches," Lily admitted.

"And the cookie?" The next photo in his hand showed a close-up of a small chunk of cookie that looked like a smaller version of a dessert cookie from the restaurant. "It could be one of mine. It's hard to tell." Lily studied the photo as she spoke.

Judy took the two photos from Detective Handler and held them at arm's length so that she and Lily could look at them side by side. One was a very clear photo of the box lunch on a table next to a napkin with a bit of cookie on it. The box was open, and a book lay on the table near the napkin. A clear glass lay on its side next to the book. The table was a faded brown with scratches and wear marks. A chair lay on its side near the table. The photo displayed two slippers resting beneath the table. The other photo showed a closer view of the partial cookie and some crumbs on the white napkin. The view over the open purple box displayed a small plastic container filled with something green beside a red and white paper-wrapped substance with the words "turkey on wheat" written on the top in black Sharpie. There was an open set of plastic wear with a salt and pepper packet inside the box as well.

"That certainly looks like one of my box lunches. I don't know what else to say." Lily said.

"Some initial testing shows that the poison was on the cookie. We will know to what degree when the lab gets back to me, but it sure looks like Mr. Creech died from eating that cookie." Detective Handler took the photos back from Judy as he made his announcement.

"The body and the cookie both testing positive for cyanide just means that someone poisoned the cookie and gave it to him in order to end his life. I guess you now need to track that cookie from its origin to the table in the picture. Mom, when would the cookie have been made if it was part of Martha Carver's order?"

"Linda made those cookies the night before the order was picked up. We ran low on cookies the day before and sold out of all the cookies from the previous batch. She prepped the cookies and the broccoli salad that night before she went home. We made the sandwiches and boxed everything the morning of pickup."

"Just you and Linda? Can you tell me Linda's last name?" The detective inquired.

"Linda Holt. She's my kitchen supervisor. She's a doll. She wouldn't hurt a fly."

"Did anyone else have access to the cookies before they left the restaurant?"

"David Grant was the only other person to come to work before Mrs. Carver picked up the order that morning. David is a nice young man. He has been cooking for me since I opened."

"I'll need contact information for both David Grant and Linda Holt, please." Detective Handler pulled a pad from his shirt pocket and started scribbling on it with a ballpoint pen.

"I guess you'll have to find out from Mrs. Carver who all could have accessed the lunches from the time she picked them up until Mr. Donavan left with the box in question. Then, it seems the box sat on Mrs. Brown's desk for a while before you left here with it." Judy looked at Jeff Donavan for confirmation.

"Yes. I carried it from the eleven o'clock meeting and dropped it on her desk until I left to go see my uncle. I stopped at my house to pick up some paperwork I had left there the night before, and then I went to see Uncle Norman. He doesn't eat regularly. I try to stop by around mealtimes to make sure he has something decent to eat. I'm not surprised that he had only eaten the cookie. He doesn't feel like eating most of the time, but he still likes his sweets now and then."

Detective Handler looked down at his pinging phone. "Confirmed. Cyanide in the cookie. Based on what they found in the cookie remains, there would have been enough poison in one cookie to kill someone. I already talked with Mrs. Carver. The boxes never left her sight before the luncheon. No one would have been able to contaminate any of them without her noticing."

"No one except Mrs. Carver," Judy added. "I'm just saying. We can't rule anyone out at this point."

"I'll do the ruling out," Jim Handler directed. "You two paid your respects. I'll let you know what the lab finds in the samples they took from the restaurant. Until then, I'd appreciate you both staying out of this investigation. Even if we rule out the restaurant ingredients, that won't rule out the possibility that someone from your place poisoned that cookie before it left the restaurant. I'll need to talk with David and Linda, and I'll be looking into motives for the three of you. You certainly had access and opportunity."

"Mom, David, Linda, Jeff, Mrs. Brown, everyone in this office, and anyone who may have been at Mr. Creech's house after Jeff dropped off the box. You sure do have a pile of suspects to wade through."

"Mr. Creech was found by the bug guy the day he ate the cookie," Detective Handler stated. "As far as we know, no one else was in the house after Jeff Donavan left."

"The bug guy? What does that mean?" Lily asked.

"The exterminator. He comes once a quarter to spray the yard," Jeff explained. "I noticed some beetles of some kind in the house last week, so I asked them to spray inside when they came. The bug guy went to the door to knock. There was no answer. He could see Uncle Norman from the back window. Appearing 'lifeless' at the table, as he put it. He called for an ambulance, and then he called me."

"I understand Norman Creech was a wealthy man. Who stands to inherit his estate?" Judy wondered out loud.

"I haven't seen his will, but I am likely one of two next of kin," Jeff stated.

"Who is the other surviving relative?" Judy asked.

"I'm Norman's late wife's nephew. Norman had another nephew who may still be alive. I haven't seen him since he moved to Idaho some years ago. He didn't keep in touch with me or my aunt and uncle. I know you think that makes us the prime suspects, but there would have been no reason to kill Norman over his money. He was dying of liver disease. He wasn't expected to be around much longer. If I were in his will, I wouldn't need to kill him to get his money. He wasn't long for this world anyway."

"What about this relative in Idaho? Did he know that?" Judy went on.

"Ladies. I'm looking into all of this. You needn't concern yourselves with the details. Rest assured. I know how to run an investigation," Detective Handler spoke more sternly now.

"I doubt Ralph, my cousin in Idaho, knows anything about Norman's will or that he was sick," Jeff answered in spite of Detective Handler's comments.

"If you'll excuse us, ladies. I have a few more details to cover with the office staff here. I'll get back to you when I know about the lab results." The detective motioned towards the door.

"Okay. Okay." Judy decided she had pushed enough... for now. "One more thing... what about the glass in the picture. Was there any trace of cyanide on the glass?"

"Goodbye, Miss Pine. I'll be in touch." Detective Handler was growing impatient with Judy.

6

—·—

"Thank you for giving me a ride home, Lily," Doug said as they sat next to each other in her Toyota Highlander.

Lily started the SUV. "No problem at all. I don't think you could drive a car with that busted-up leg, even if you had a car. I will say that you look much better today. I trust you feel better."

"Yes. The doc fixed me up and gave me some great pain meds. I'll be laid up for a while. I talked with Handler. He told me your restaurant was cleared by the lab."

"He called me early this morning. Linda and Chase are getting ready to open for lunch. No cookies for now." She raised her eyebrows, glancing over at Doug.

"Jim also told me that they found traces of poison in the puddle of milk on the floor. They are checking the contents of the refrigerator to see if anything else was tainted."

"He didn't check the milk initially? He may only be checking it now because Judy asked about the overturned glass next to the cookie on the table. Shouldn't they have checked that from the get-go?"

"Jim Handler sometimes decides what happened and chases down his theory instead of collecting everything and then letting the evidence tell the story. He likes to pick the most likely suspect and then prove they did it. Not my method but this is his case."

"Is it possible the killer poisoned several other items at the house in addition to the cookie in an effort to increase their odds of killing him?"

"Possible but seems unlikely since the cookie had just arrived a few hours before the body was found. Maybe he dipped the cookie in the milk, leaving some residual poison from the cookie in the milk. As he struggled from the poison, he likely knocked the glass over and spilled the milk. More evidence will need to be collected to understand for sure."

"Did he mention alibies or motives? It appears that Jeff Donavan has the most to gain, but according to him, Norman Creech was going to die soon anyway. So, why would anyone bother killing a man who was already knocking on death's door? It seems like a lot of risk just to speed up the inevitable."

"I'm sure Jim is checking Jeff's financial information to see if he needed money in a hurry for some reason. That would be my first thought."

"Interesting that you bring that up. Judy is researching Jeff Donavan's business affairs as we speak." Lily grinned without taking her eyes off the road.

"I'm sure she will find the long-lost cousin as well." Doug started to laugh.

"She's also checking out all the staff at the accounting firm as well as looking into Mrs. Carver. They all had access to the box lunch after it left the restaurant. She will be double-checking the backgrounds of our staff involved, too. I know I haven't known them long, but I can't imagine any of my team members had a hand in this."

"There isn't always a direct motive. Sometimes a murderer is paid to kill someone they don't even know. I once convicted a killer who followed a guy home and shot him for cutting him off on the highway. Anything is possible."

"I bet it was hard to connect the dots on that one."

"I didn't solve it overnight, that's for sure. It could be that Creech just ticked off a neighbor, or he had an old girlfriend with a jealous husband who waited years to make his move. Following the evidence is the only way to find the answer."

Lily helped Doug get into his wheelchair and then into his living room. He assured her he was okay alone, and she left him so that she could get back to Poulsbo and check on the restaurant.

7

After the lunch rush, Lily went home to care for her Petit Basset Griffon Vendéen, Nellie. Nellie was a happy dog who showed her emotions with a full-body wag. Lily scratched the shaggy dog's head and then offered her fresh water and a small bowl of dry dog food. Nellie finished about half of the food and then posed near the door until Lily joined her with a leash. After a brisk walk, they arrived home to find Judy at the condo.

"Hey, Mom. How was your walk?"

"We had a grand time. Nellie got to sniff a Great Dane. We ran into Renee Valentine and her father. She's a hoot, and he is quite interesting to talk to as well. They brought up Mr. Creech. They knew he had died but didn't seem to have any details. I don't think they knew he was poisoned... which is good. That means the detective hasn't leaked the information about the cookie. Apparently, back in the day, Mr. Valentine did business with Mr. Creech. He said he hadn't seen him in years. What have you been up to?"

"I've been researching everyone who might have had access to that cookie. It doesn't seem likely that Jeff Donavan was in desperate need of money. He seems to lead a fairly modest life. Everybody wants more though, you know."

"What about the cousin?"

"Ralph Creech lived in Boise, Idaho but moved to Portland a few years ago. He has a nice house and a small construction business. Nothing very interesting there. I wish we knew the contents of Norman's will. Maybe if we knew who was getting all his money, we'd have a better idea of who would benefit most from his death. I'm unsure what else could be a motive for killing the guy, though no one has spoken very highly of him. Maybe he just rubbed the wrong person the wrong way. Since he was dying, killing him seems a little pointless unless the killer didn't know he was dying."

"How about Mrs. Carver's charity? Do you think someone may be upset with Creech for not giving his bountiful fortune?"

"I guess Mrs. Carver could be upset that they weren't able to convince Norman to help with their cause. She supports cancer research. Perhaps the lack of funds has caused personal grief for her in some way. I'll keep digging into her personal life. There could be something there. I'd like to go back to Jeff's office and talk to the staff. Everyone there had access to the box lunch, and Mrs. Brown, for one, did not seem to like Mr. Creech at all. Maybe everyone there felt the same way. Maybe one of them hated him enough to kill him. Did Doug get back to you with any news about tests on any other food in the house at Norman's or any other evidence that might help narrow this down?"

"He found out there were traces of poison in the milk. They think it may have gotten in the milk by Creech dunking the cookie."

"Clearing up what happened before news of the poison gets out will surely help people feel better about eating your cookies."

"We aren't selling cookies for now. Just in case it gets out. I don't want people thinking about it. We might give the cookies a rest for a while even after this blows over."

"That's a shame. Those cookies are so great. Hey, what if Doug is wrong?"

"About what?"

"What if he's right about the cross-contamination from the cookie being dunked in milk but wrong about where the poison came from? Suppose the milk was tainted, and he soaked the cookie in milk as he ate it. The poison could have been in the milk, and he transferred it to the cookie."

"How would we be able to prove that if it were true?"

"If Handler is doing his job and tests the milk from the refrigerator, they may find out that is the source of the poison."

"That would change the entire investigation. If the milk is the origin of the poison, who had access to the box lunch is irrelevant. I'd feel a lot better knowing he didn't die from the cookie, no matter how the poison may have gotten into it."

"Maybe you should call Doug and plant the idea in his head. Ask him to mention it to Handler. We want to make sure he considers the idea while getting to take credit for it himself. I'll try to figure out where Norman shops and when he last purchased milk."

"How are you going to do that?"

"I have no idea, but I'll come up with something."

"Okay. I wanted to check in on Doug anyway. I'll give him a call."

"Thanks, Mom. How about we take a road trip tomorrow? It's your day off, right?"

"Yes. I was planning to have dinner with Jed. Where would we take a road trip to?"

"Portland. I thought we could visit Portland, Oregon. Cousin Ralph lives in Portland now."

"Instead of trying to talk you out of it, I'll just agree to go as long as you get me back here in time for dinner."

"Deal."

8

"Hi. Are you Ralph Creech?" Judy approached the large man in the white hard hat. They stood about a block from a building under construction. Judy and Lily had just pulled up when Ralph exited his Ford F150. He was walking towards the construction site with a set of blueprints tucked under his arm.

"For a pretty lady like you, I am." Ralph smiled broadly at Judy through crooked teeth and then spit across the sidewalk. Tobacco filled his left cheek.

"I'm Judy, and this is Lily," Judy said as she glanced back toward her mother.

"What can I do for you ladies?" He gave Judy a quick wink.

"We were hoping to ask you about Norman Creech," Judy replied, taking a step back.

"Old Uncle Norman. I haven't seen him in years. What about him?" Ralph turned and spit again.

"Are you aware that he passed away recently?" Judy went on.

"Actually, a detective from Washington called me about that very thing. He told me Uncle Norman had been poisoned. I asked him if he considered that the old man may have done himself in. He wasn't a well man. I believe he expected to die soon anyway."

"So, you knew about his liver disease?" Judy wanted to clarify.

"Yes. I haven't seen Norman in several years, but he called me a few weeks ago out of the blue. He seemed to want to reminisce about family and old times. Since I didn't remember him being the nostalgic type, I asked him where this was all coming from. He told me he was dying. He always was a peculiar little man. Not a nice man either. He could have made any number of people mad enough to want to kill him, I suppose. At least, that's how I remember him."

"I don't think it's odd for someone who knows they are dying to reach out to family or to want to talk about their loved ones," Lily spoke softly but sternly, with her brows tensed.

"Have you been to Port Townsend recently? Have you been in touch with Jeff Donavan?" Judy continued her line of questioning.

"No and no. Not that it's any of your business. Jeff and I are barely acquainted. I haven't talked to him in years. I have to get to work. You two will excuse me," He stated more than requested and walked away from Judy and Lily.

"He's not very polite," Lily whispered.

"No. He isn't a pleasant man. Maybe he gets the attitude from Uncle Norman's side of the family. That would explain why people didn't like the man. If he knew Norman Creech was dying, he wouldn't have any reason to poison him even if he is in the will. This whole thing has got me stumped. I thought for sure his money was the best motive, but his only relatives knew he was dying. Maybe someone else is named in the will. Maybe someone killed him because they thought he was mean like Ralph said."

"Or maybe Norman Creech did kill himself. That was a long drive for a very brief conversation," Lily commented to her daughter.

"Yes, but he may not have spoken to us over the phone. It's harder to disregard someone when you are face to face with them."

"He wouldn't have seen how pretty you are over the phone," Lily laughed as she spoke.

"And I wouldn't have been able to tell how charming he is." Judy laughed along.

Lily's phone chimed, and she looked down to see a text from Doug. *The milk carton contained a high level of sodium cyanide. The poison seems to have originated in the milk.*

9

⸺ ✦ ⸺

J udy and Lily parked behind the only five cars they saw along the cemetery drive, one of which being a long gray hearse. Dressed in similar black dresses, the two ladies exited the Highlander and neared the small group of people standing at the gravesite. Martha Carver and Kathryn Brown flanked Jeff Donavan near the ornate casket. Lily was surprised to see David Gant and Ken Valentine standing behind Jeff. From what David had said at the restaurant, Lily didn't think David knew Norman Creech well and didn't seem to think much of him. Judy was curious to know more about the relationship between Mr. Creech and Mr. Valentine. With the small turnout for the graveside funeral, she wondered why these were the people who attended. She assumed the two women standing with Jeff were merely there to support him. Without a word, Lily and Judy rounded the group and stood behind everyone except for the preacher, who faced everyone from the opposite side of a freshly dug grave.

The preacher spoke for several minutes before the casket was lowered into the grave. Jeff stepped forward to scoop dirt into the grave in a ceremonial fashion. The group remained silent as Jeff continued to look down. Mrs. Brown and Mrs. Carver stepped forward with Jeff, gripping each of his arms. Judy and Lily turned to watch Ken Valentine walk slowly to his car. Ken passed another man who hadn't been in the cemetery when the sermon started. He had not stood within earshot of the somber ceremony. Lily and Judy only noticed him when they turned their heads to watch Mr. Valentine walk away. It was Ralph Creech. He stood near the line of parked cars, but his truck was not in sight. Before Mr. Valentine could reach him, Ralph turned and walked away.

The preacher offered a few parting words and the group dispersed towards their cars.

Lily called out to her cook, "David. I didn't expect to see you here."

"I am surprised to see you here as well, Lily." He turned to face his boss and her daughter. "I didn't think you actually knew the deceased."

"We didn't, but we thought we should pay our respects, under the circumstances," Judy offered.

"I wanted to see who would show up for Norman's funeral," Judy admitted. "Why are you here?"

"My grandmother would have wanted me to come. She was fond of Mr. Creech. Most people around town didn't like the man, but she thought he was misunderstood. She grew up with him. Grandma would say that he wasn't always the grumpy man people judged him for. She and Norman were quite the couple back in the day. They dated when they were teenagers and though they separated and married other people, they stayed friends up until her death. I didn't know Norman Creech very well. Most people thought of him as an unkind man. I only came here today in honor of my grandmother."

"That's very noble of you David," Lily said.

"What about Ken Valentine?" Judy asked. "Do you know why he was compelled to be here today? He left before I had a chance to talk with him."

"I believe Ken Valentine and Norman Creech worked together from time to time. I think they had business dealings. I am unsure of their personal relationship. Will you be at the restaurant tonight, Lily?"

"I'll be there briefly for a check-in, but Linda is running the show tonight. Do you work this evening?" Lily asked.

"Yes." He responded. "I really should go. I'm due at the restaurant soon. I'll need to get changed and get to work. I'll call Linda if I think I'll be running late."

"Good idea. She'll understand but will likely worry if she doesn't hear from you." Lily said.

"Thank you, Lily. Goodbye, Judy." The young man stepped briskly to his car and left the cemetery. The Highlander was the only car, other than the hearse, that remained.

"Pretty sorry turnout wouldn't you say?" Judy shook her head as they got into the large SUV.

"Yes. Considering that he has lived in the area for decades, I expected more people to attend his funeral. I know you thought the killer was likely to show up for the funeral. If that's the case, we have surely trimmed down the pool of suspects."

"I feel like we have increased the number of possible killers. I hadn't considered Mrs. Brown and Mrs. Carver, David, or Mr. Valentine."

"Just because they were here doesn't mean they are suspects. What would their motives be?"

"Mrs. Brown didn't like the way Norman treated Jeff. Mrs. Carver could feel the same way. We only have a glimpse of the relationships Norman had with Ken Valentine and David's grandmother. I bet there's much more to those stories."

"Now that we know the poison was in the milk, we know David didn't poison the cookie before it left the restaurant."

"That doesn't mean he didn't have a chance to add cyanide to the milk in Norman Creech's refrigerator somehow. How well do you know David? Do you think he could have done something like this? Can you imagine him being a killer?"

"David has worked for me since I opened the restaurant. He is a hard worker and a good friend. He is very jovial, and the staff love working with him. He and Chase go out together quite often. No. I can't imagine he would hurt anyone."

"Not even for his grandmother? I bet there's more to that story. A lonely widow never getting over the man she loved in her youth. Something like that." Judy loved a good backstory.

"David's grandmother practically raised him. His parents died when he was young. I forget the circumstances. He speaks highly of his grandmother. I believe she passed away a couple of years ago. I don't see any reason why that would be any reason to kill Norman Creech. I don't think David is capable of such actions."

"What do you make of Mr. Valentine being here? Do you know what kind of business relationship he and Norman had?"

"I don't know much about Ken Valentine. I spend time with his daughter, Renee, occasionally, but we don't talk about her father much. We don't usually talk about anything of much substance. Light conversation and cocktails are usually the order of business with Renee. I understand from her that Ken is retired now. I'm not sure what type of business he was in or why he would have had a business relationship with Mr. Creech."

"Do you think you could arrange for us to meet with Ken Valentine? I'd like to see where that story leads. If nothing else, it may be an interesting addition to my article once this case is all wrapped up."

"I'll try to contact him through Renee. We have become pretty close. She's rarely too busy to meet for a drink," Lily responded with a soft chuckle.

"Did you notice Ralph lurking about?"

"I didn't notice him until Ken Valentine made his exit. It's interesting that he didn't join the small group at the gravesite."

"Ralph does seem a bit antisocial, and he doesn't strike me as the sentimental type. After our conversation with him in Portland, I didn't expect to see him here."

"Agreed. He didn't seem to care one way or another that Norman had passed away. He sure doesn't seem like the type to show up out of etiquette." Lily laughed.

"I doubt he knows what that word means," Judy smirked.

10

Jed Stride walked along the main retail area of downtown Poulsbo loosely holding the leash of his adorable, apricot colored Goldendoodle. The curly-haired dog was tall but walked with his head down, shifting it from side to side to soak up the smells of the sidewalk and plants along the way. Brick and Jed were scheduled to meet Nellie and Lily for dinner at an outside sitting area near the walk-up window for Jed's favorite burrito place in town. Lily and Jed often met at this dog-friendly spot to share a meal with their dogs in attendance.

"Hi, Jed," Lily said. "I'm sorry we're late."

"We just got here as well. We were running a bit behind schedule too. Not Brick's fault. He was ready on time. I was late getting finished with work. The produce business is booming. I was glad to see your order back to normal today. You must be confident that the story about the poisoning in Port Townsend hasn't gotten around like you expected."

Brick sniffed Nellie politely as she wagged her body for several seconds before laying down next to the table. Brick slumped into a reclining position as well, stretching his chin to within an inch of Nellie's. The two dogs rested contently at each other's side while the two humans talked.

"As it turns out, the man wasn't poisoned by the cookie but rather by the milk he dunked his cookie in. Doug said the milk in the refrigerator was full of cyanide. The forensic team is convinced that the carton of milk is the sole source of the poison. The investigator has kept the entire thing pretty hush-hush, so I don't think the media has picked it up yet. As far as the Seattle paper goes, I have an in with the investigating reporter who works the peninsula beat."

"That helps, I'm sure. I assumed people in town would wonder about why you were closed for dinner the other night."

"We had a few inquiries, but we offered only vague reasons for being closed. Hopefully, by the time word gets around about it being linked to someone's death, the full story should be out, and it will confirm that our food was not to blame."

"That's good to hear. Do they know how the milk was poisoned or who did the poisoning?"

"Not that I am aware of. The detective on the case was pretty set on blaming us. Now that the milk has been deemed the true source of the cyanide, he's having to start over. He's trying to figure out who had access to Norman Creech's refrigerator or how it might have been dosed at the store. Doug has shared some information with me, but I don't think Detective Handler is sharing everything with him. Doug is supposed to be off-duty."

"Oh, yes. How is Detective Miller? I heard he was in a terrible accident."

"He's doing very well for a man who was run over by a truck," Lily smiled as she spoke. "He is in some pain but otherwise in good shape. He should make a full recovery. At least he is home from the hospital now."

"That's good to hear."

Jed and Lily got together on a fairly regular basis, and Jed knew Lily also shared meals with Doug Miller from time to time, but they didn't talk about it. Lily liked having both of the men as friends and hoped that neither would become uncomfortable about her seeing the other. She never lied to either of them and didn't keep it a secret that she spent time with both of them. Neither of the men brought it up as a problem, and everyone seemed happy with the way the friendships were going. Everyone was cordial on occasions when they all ran into one another somewhere on the peninsula.

Lily smiled at the two dogs laying side by side with their chins on the ground, merely inches apart. "Aren't they sweet?"

"They certainly are. Nellie is pretty cute and friendly. They seem very comfortable together. I think Brick looks forward to his time with her."

As Jed smiled at Lily, she thought he was using the dogs as a metaphor for how he felt about her. She hoped he was, at least. Her eyes shined with happiness.

11

⸺ ❖ ⸻

"Good morning, Jeff," Lily greeted Mr. Donavan as they entered the office overlooking Port Townsend Bay.

"Thank you for asking us here to talk about your uncle's will." Judy had kind of invited herself. She didn't tell her mom that.

"Oh, yes. I'm happy to have you both here. The executor was asked to hurry up the probate process so that the detective could find out what information Uncle Norman's will might lend to the case. Mr. Elder is the executor. He told me I could get copy quicker by meeting him here today. You seem to be very helpful in the investigation, so I thought you should get to hear what it says as soon as possible." Jeff blushed a little as Judy smiled at him.

"Isn't there going to be a reading of the will? Is your cousin coming?" Lily raised her eyebrows in an excited fashion.

"Oh, Mom. That only happens in the movies. The executor just releases the notice that the will has been probated and sends a copy." Judy informed her mother.

"Yes. Mr. Elder called me. He's an old friend of the family. Norman named him executor of his estate years ago. He said I could pick up the official paperwork and the will here to save waiting for the mail," Jeff said to the ladies.

A door at the far end of the office opened and a tall, lean man with grey hair wearing a three-piece suit entered. Before he could speak, the door nearest Jeff and the ladies also opened, and Detective Handler walked through the doorway.

"Detective Handler. You are just in time. I was about to present Mr. Donavan with the will." Mr. Elder spoke loudly and with an official tone. He placed several documents on the long ornate table in the center of the large room. "Everyone, please have a seat. Mr. Donavan, I will need you to sign here and here." Mr. Elder tapped near the bottom of two of the documents he had spread out on the table.

"What are you two doing here?" Detective Handler asked as he took a seat across from the two ladies.

"Mr. Donavan invited us. Why are you here?" Judy asked smugly.

"I invited him as well. You are all so intent on figuring out what happened to my uncle; I wanted you to hear what was in the will right away. I know my uncle was destined to die soon, but I think it is despicable that some evil person saw fit to rob him of his final days. If there is something in this document that might help you figure out who would do such a thing, I want you to be fully informed." Jeff signed the papers and dropped the pen on the table.

"Here you go." Mr. Elder handed a thick document to Jeff Donavan and scooped up the signed papers.

Mr. Elder sat down at the head of the table, and Jeff sat to his immediate left, next to Judy. Jim Handler glared at Judy from across the table. Lily leaned back in the chair next to Judy and looked past Jim to the seagull that rested on a dock post outside the window. She looked out the window, wishing they weren't about to hear the last wishes of a man who died too early. She took a moment of peace in the gentle roll of the water in the bay.

As Jeff started to read the document, his lips moved softly, but he spoke in only a whisper. The others couldn't make out what he was saying. Judy and Jim leaned forward on their elbows as Jeff turned the first page and continued reading to himself. He continued to turn pages but didn't say anything aloud for several minutes. Finally, he dropped the papers to the table and looked at Mr. Elder. "I had no idea. I mean... I knew he was wealthy, but this is a ridiculous amount of money. He never told me."

"He left the bulk of his estate to you, Mr. Donavan," Mr. Elder said as he stared at Jeff. "Norman and Laura set the trust up years ago. They each became the owners of the estate in the event of the other's death. You were named in the document as the successor in the event that anything happened to both of them. It was your aunt's idea. God rest her soul. They also named your cousin Ralph in the will. I sent his paperwork out this morning. He will get a copy of the whole thing, just like you did."

"Yes. I see that. It looks like there is a rental property on the bay that Norman left to Ralph. My aunt Laura once told me Norman used to take her and Ralph kayaking at that property in the summer. As long as I've known Norman, he has rented it out to tourists. He has kept it in decent shape."

"Is that all he left to Ralph," Judy asked as if it were any of her business.

"Yes," Mr. Elder responded. "I asked Norman if he wanted to update the will once Laura died, but he never got around to it. He had a hard time with Laura's death, and he didn't care much what happened to his estate once she was gone."

"It sounds like old Mr. Creech had a soft spot," Lily offered.

"He had a soft spot for Laura, all right. That old grump was putty in her hands. He was a totally different person around her. Laura never thought he was abrasive or mean. She saw him in a completely different light." Jeff looked towards the ceiling as if he could see Laura above him. "He was a different man with her. He was sweet and caring towards her. She was a beautiful person, inside and out."

"I don't see that this helps our case any," Detective Handler said, scratching his chin. "Jeff here was the main heir to Creech's fortune, and he was in line to get that whether the old man died of liver disease, poisoning, or anything else. It doesn't seem like much of a motive. Ralph had no reason to murder him since he was only getting that one piece of property, and from what you ladies said, he knew Creech was dying of liver disease as well."

"Unless there was some reason Ralph Creech needed access to that property in a hurry," Judy speculated.

"For what kind of reason?" Lily asked.

"I don't know. I'm just thinking out loud. Since the only two people who stood to gain anything from Norman's death already knew he was going to die soon, it doesn't seem likely that they had anything to do with the poisoning unless they had some reason to hurry the process."

"It seems to me that we need to start looking for another motive. Norman Creech wasn't well-liked in this town. It's extremely possible that he made someone angry enough to want him dead. People are killed for the craziest reasons." Detective Handler moved towards the exit. "I appreciate you letting me come here to hear all of this, but I have a case to crack." He nodded at Jeff and Mr. Elder and left the building.

Judy sat down at the long table and looked over at Jeff. "Do you mind if I take a look at these documents?"

"Not at all," Jeff replied as he pushed the pile of papers toward her.

"Mr. Elder. Will it take long to get this all taken care of? Once I have access to the funds, I have a number of charities I'd like to share Norman's money with."

"We should have this all wrapped up in a few days at this point. I can handle the transfer of funds for you," Mr. Elder responded.

"I guess Norman Creech will become a charitable man after all," Lily said with a subtle grin.

"He might be rolling over in his grave," Jeff added.

As Judy sifted through the papers in front of her, she looked up at Jeff. "Did you hear the lab results show that the poison likely came from the milk and not the cookie?"

"Yes, Detective Handler already questioned me about where Norman did his shopping. He gets everything delivered from the local market near his house. I believe the detective had all the milk pulled off the shelf, and they are reviewing the source and transportation," he responded as she shifted her attention back toward the documents at her fingertips.

"It's turning into a bit of a wild goose chase," Lily shook her head and sat down next to her daughter. "It's like the Tylenol murders that happened in Chicago back in the early eighties."

"I wrote an article related to that once. You know they never actually solved that crime," Judy said without looking up. "They confirmed that the tampering happened after the Tylenol was in the store. That could be the case here. Perhaps someone just contaminated one carton of milk to cause a random death."

"I thought they caught the Tylenol guy. He tried to blackmail the drug company," Lily said.

"They didn't have enough evidence to prove he was responsible for the poisoning, but he *was* convicted of extortion. We should go." Judy pushed the stack of documents back towards Jeff and got up from the table.

"I hope the search for the truth doesn't turn out like the Tylenol thing," Mr. Elder chimed in. "That was devastating for the Johnson & Johnson company at the time. It was devastating for the community as well."

12

———— ◆ ————

Lily and Judy sat together on one side of a booth in a café in Poulsbo's main shopping district. The café was bustling even though it was ten in the morning. Virgil was ringing the order bell, and Annie was hustling through the dining room with two pots of coffee, offering refills. She dropped two mugs on the table in front of Judy and Lily Pine and filled their cups with regular. "Anything else for now?" Annie asked.

"We are expecting the Valentines to join us. We'll wait to order if that's okay." Lily looked apologetic.

Annie moved on to the next table in a hurried fashion without a word. She smiled and nodded as she moved away. She topped off a few more coffee cups and grabbed some heaping plates of food from the order window. Sizzling and chopping sounds could be heard from the order window, allowing Lily to picture Virgil working away in the back.

The silver bell at the top of the entrance rang out, and Judy looked towards the door. Renee Valentine approached the two ladies in a bright yellow raincoat that stopped halfway between her waist and her knees. Her long legs were bare below the dripping wet coat. Her feet rested in a pair of bling-covered sandals. Judy noted that she wasn't the only patron watching Renee strut into the café. As Renee shook her umbrella at the door and closed it tightly, she smiled a bright, red-lipped smile at several of the men at the counter, raising one trim eyebrow as she passed them to slide into the booth across from Judy and Lily. Somehow her hair looked perfect despite the weather.

"Hello, ladies," she said with a cat-like grin.

"You do make an entrance," Lily said, smiling back at her.

"Don't you think people would be disappointed if I didn't?" Renee laughed.

Judy rolled her eyes and shook her head with a subtle grin. "Where's your dad? I was hoping to talk to him as well."

"Oh, you know Daddy. He likes to stay home when it rains. He doesn't get out much. He keeps talking about moving to Arizona. He says he hates the rain, but he's lived in the Pacific Northwest his entire life. He's so funny." Renee took off her shiny coat and stuffed it into the corner of the bench seat. She wore bright yellow shorts and a tightly fitted black top.

"I was hoping to ask him about Mr. Creech," Judy confessed.

"That old buzzard. Daddy wouldn't have anything nice to say about him. It's probably a good thing he didn't come along."

"When I saw the two of you the other day, your father said he had business dealings with Norman Creech. He didn't mention that there were any ill feelings," Lily recalled.

"You know how he is. He tries to speak well of people and say the proper thing. I don't know how long he'd hold his tongue about old Norman though if you asked directly. As I understand it, Norman promised to back Daddy up, financially, in a big property venture years ago. Norman backed out of the deal at the last minute, leaving egg on Daddy's face and costing him a fortune in the eventual proceeds that would have transpired from the deal. Daddy has told me more than once that he'd be a millionaire today if it weren't for Norman Creech backing out on their deal. To top it off, Creech bought some of the property on his own and made a bundle."

"It sounds like your father had good reason to hate Mr. Creech," Judy said.

"To put it mildly," Renee replied. "Why are you interested in Norman Creech? I understand he's dead. Hey, do you know who got all his money?"

"There is reason to believe there was foul play involved in Norman's death." Lily felt a little bad for not leading with that.

"Oh, come on. Are you telling me someone may have killed that old devil? My father isn't capable of such a thing, but I'm sure there is a long line of people who are just as happy to hear that guy is dead. Any number of people have reason to dislike Mr. Creech. He's been around this area for decades, stepping on other people to make his fortune."

"Can you name a few?" Judy was ready to make mental notes of anyone who may have a motive.

"Pick any businessman on the peninsula and they likely had a run-in with Norman Creech. I understand his nephew isn't to be trusted either." Renee shook her head at Annie as she approached with the coffee pot and another mug. Annie walked on by.

"Jeff?" Lily asked.

"I don't think that's his name. I don't remember. He has moved around quite a bit. He's in construction but known to cut corners, so he keeps moving to a different state," Renee went on.

"Oh, that's probably Ralph Creech," Judy expressed.

"Yes. That sounds right. I hear he's a mess, just like his uncle. Did you just ask us here to try to pin this would-be murder on my father?"

"Oh, no. We had no idea your father didn't like Mr. Creech. We were just hoping to get some background... you know... history on the man. He mentioned he knew Norman, and then we saw your father at Norman's funeral." Lily stammered a little. She felt bad for seeming to trap Renee in such a conversation.

"It's okay, Hon." Renee winked at Lily. "I'm not offended. But you are going to buy me brunch, right?"

"Judy is." Lily gave out a relaxed laugh.

Renee motioned for Annie to come back to the table.

"Daddy goes to everyone's funeral. Well, everyone he knows. He always says, 'It's the right thing to do.' I think he's afraid no one will show up for him when the time comes. He wants to make sure that doesn't happen to anyone else."

"Mimosa, easy on the OJ, Renee?" Annie asked.

"You know me so well," Renee responded as her cat-like grin returned.

13

As the sun set on Port Townsend, the snowcapped mountains seemed to glow at the water's edge. The bay was smooth and quiet. The rain had stopped for the time being, and Lily was walking along the dock, enjoying a bit of sun breaking through the clouds along the horizon. She sometimes wondered if she would ever tire of the enchanting views that this area of the country offered. She couldn't imagine ever taking them for granted.

"Hey, Lily, thanks for coming." Jeff Donavan approached Lily from the ferry parking lot. "Where's Judy?"

"I'm sorry; she couldn't make it. She had a date with a dog. Your text said you wanted to talk about the 'milk and cookies,' so I thought I should go ahead and meet you."

"I was trying to be cute. I guess that was a bit cryptic. It's really about my cousin, Ralph. He's here in Port Townsend. He plans to contest the will. He claims Norman was going to change his will and leave everything to him. I have already promised most of the money to the cancer charity. I can't tell Mrs. Carver that I can't give it to her. She's counting on me. Ralph also asked the current renters at the property he inherited to leave in the middle of their stay. He offered to reimburse them their entire rent amount."

"Why does he need to get on the property so quickly?"

"I don't know. Maybe there is something on it he wants. I also found out he was here in Port Townsend the day Norman died. He was on the rental property that day as well. He's up to something."

"Judy asked him if he had been here, and he said he hadn't. We heard he isn't to be trusted. A friend of ours told us he has moved from state to state to elude the people he has cheated in his business dealings."

"Sounds a lot like Norman except Norman didn't care about living amongst the people he swindled. He had very little in the way of scruples."

"If you thought so little of him, why did you spend so much time taking care of him? Mrs. Carver told us you checked in on him at least once every day."

"My aunt loved him so much. She worried about what would happen to him if she were to die before he did. She once asked me to promise to take care of him in the event that happened. I had to fulfill my promise to her. I moved here several years ago to be closer to Aunt Laura. She was delightful. I wish you could have known her. Sadly, she died in a tragic accident. She was my only blood relative. I couldn't let her down."

"That's very noble of you. Did Norman treat you well?"

"I wouldn't say he was nice, but he was civil to me. He didn't seem to care about much of anything since her death. He never spoke of her, but I think he was lost without Aunt Laura."

"That was months ago, wasn't it?"

"Yes. Coming up on one year. Next week will be the first anniversary of her death."

"I'm sorry. I'm sure this is a hard time for you. Is there something you were hoping Judy and I could help you with? Is there a particular reason why you asked us here?"

"You two seem to have good intuition about what is going on in the case. I'm not sure Detective Handler has a clue what he's doing. I was hoping you two could look into the property and help me figure out why Ralph is so intent on getting on the premises. He's likely there now. Do you have any idea how we might go about finding out what he's doing there?"

"I'm not the one to ask. My daughter is the investigative reporter. I'm just a restaurant owner."

"I heard you figured out who killed a guy in your building last year. You are one for one, which is a better close rate than the detective from what I hear."

"Do you think Mrs. Carver knew that you would donate money to her if you inherited it from your uncle's estate?"

"I'm not sure, but it's likely. I have been an avid supporter of her cause. It would be a reasonable assumption. Why do you ask?"

"Just wondering."

14

_____ ❋ _____

"Hi, Doug. I'm driving back from Port Townsend. I wanted to check on you to see how you're doing." Lily spoke over the speakerphone in her SUV.

"That's very nice of you." Doug tried to sit up on his sofa, shaking off the drowsiness from his pain medication the best he could.

"So. How are you doing?"

"I'm as good as can be expected. You know, anytime someone cuts you open, there's going to be some pain."

"Are you taking your pain meds?"

"I skipped them last night because they were making me feel nauseous. It turns out the pain is worse than the nausea, so I'm back on them. They make me a bit groggy, too."

"You should take them and stay on the couch for the next few days. Can I bring you anything?"

"No. I'm okay. Officer Crum from Gig Harbor brought a couple of sandwiches for me. He wanted to ask a few more questions about the crash. He's not so sure it was an accident."

"What does that mean? I thought you were hit by a semitruck."

"I was. It was a hit-and-run. Pete Crum has been assigned to the case. He's trying to track the driver down. Based on the evidence at the scene, he's pretty sure the person driving the truck meant to hit me. I was about to get off the bridge on the north side when it happened. I didn't see it coming. I was thinking about the case I was driving towards, and then all of a sudden, there was a huge impact. I woke up at the hospital."

"Did they check for a head injury?"

"Yes. The doctor said I didn't suffer any permanent damage to my head. All the excuses for stupid stuff I do, which I was looking forward to using, are out the window. My bruises and cuts will heal soon enough and so will this busted-up leg."

"Why would anyone run into you intentionally?"

"That's what Crum is working on. I wasn't much help. He's looking into everyone I've put away and anyone who has been recently released. He's got quite a list. He has some leads on the truck from some eyewitness descriptions but nothing concrete at this point. A red Kenworth semi-cab without a trailer is what he was told by a bystander who stopped to call the ambulance. There had to be some damage to the truck though I'm sure it fared much better than my car did."

"It fared well enough to drive away. I imagine you have made quite a few enemies with criminals of different types. Poor Officer Crum."

"Yes. Officer Crum has quite a list of suspects."

"Have you heard anything more from Detective Handler about the Creech case?"

"No. He hasn't contacted me at all. He likely wants me to stay out of his business. I can't blame him. I like to work my own cases to the end as well."

"You have been known to look for help and information anywhere you can get it."

"That's true, but he probably doesn't think I can help him. I think he only called me at the start of the case because he knew I was friends with you. He was looking for some inside information on the restaurant. Now that he has moved on to the milk and away from your cookie, I don't hold the same value to him."

"Any thoughts on how the milk was altered?"

"Several. The facts have to be followed to get to the correct answer. Handler needs to keep looking and following the evidence."

"If there is anything I can do for you, please don't hesitate to ask."

"Thank you. I won't."

"You get some rest."

"Yes, ma'am."

15

—— ❖ ——

"Did you get the puppy?" was Lily's first question as she answered the phone.

"He was pretty cute, but I'm still undecided. Am I ready to take care of a puppy?" Judy asked.

"You will be surprised how a sweet dog can fill your life with love."

"I told the rescue place I'd be back. They have three puppies. One of them laid his little chin on my shoulder when I picked him up. He was so sweet. They won't be old enough to leave her for another week. I'll make a decision by more then." Judy said with a grin. "Hearing about your conversation with Jeff Donavan, I decided to go back to Port Townsend and talk with some of Jeff's co-workers and Mrs. Carver. No one at the accounting office had anything nice to say about Norman Creech. Mrs. Brown was especially upset while talking about him. She told me a few stories about Mr. Creech making demands on Jeff. She claims that Jeff bent over backward to please the old man but got nothing but grief in return."

"Did she witness the abuse firsthand?"

"It didn't seem so. Most of the accounts were as told by Jeff. Mr. Creech didn't leave his house much, according to what everyone at Jeff's office said. He had become a bit of a hermit."

"I'm not surprised, knowing about his medical condition. It was likely uncomfortable for Mr. Creech to be out and about."

"The entire office described him as if they were depicting Ebenezer Scrooge from the Christmas story."

"Did you learn anything from Mrs. Carver? Did she give you similar feedback?"

"She did, but more interesting is the fact that she is very jubilant about the prospect of getting a sizable donation from Jeff for her charity. She had a shine in her eyes and a giddy attitude when talking about Jeff Donavan coming into the sizable fortune he would be getting from Norman's estate. She went on and on about the amount of cancer research this type of donation can support. She presented the concept as if Norman Creech's death were a good thing. She made the comment that 'it couldn't have happened at a better time,' but when I probed her on the timing, she wouldn't elaborate. For some reason, it seemed important to her that the charity would be getting the exorbitant amount of funds in the coming days."

"Interesting. I wonder if there is a particular reason for the hurry. I assume she knew Norman was dying. Do you think she had some reason to expedite his demise?"

"Even if she did, how would she have gotten access to Mr. Creech's milk? I suppose anyone could have snuck into the house and tainted the milk carton in some way. I don't know what good it will do, but I'm headed to the grocery store near Norman Creech's house now. I hope to find out who delivered his last order. It's a small local store. That makes me fairly confident I can get them to share the information with me. I called ahead, and the manager agreed to see me."

"I bet Detective Handler has already questioned the manager and the delivery person."

"I made the same assumption when I talked with the manager on the phone. He said he had not spoken to the police in person. I get the feeling Detective Handler isn't the most competent officer on the force."

"Doug said as much. He doesn't seem to have much confidence in the guy. I would think the grocery store would need to be closed down for testing, just like my restaurant was."

"How is Doug? You said you were going to check in with him yesterday."

"He seems to be doing well. At least, that is what he says. You know he isn't one to complain. Turns out, he was the victim of a hit-and-run accident."

"Really? He didn't mention that at the hospital."

"The officer in charge of the hit-and-run thinks it may have been intentional."

"Do you mean he thinks someone meant to hurt Doug?"

"Yes. He's looking into all of Doug's past cases. Apparently, he has a long list of suspects, according to Doug."

"That sounds like another great story for the paper. Maybe I can talk to the officer in charge." Judy's voice inflection increased as she got excited at the prospect of a new story.

"Talk with Doug about it before you go sticking your nose in, okay?"

"I will. I promise not to print anything about Doug without talking with him first."

"*Police Detective Narrowly Escapes Killer on Narrows Bridge* sounds like a great headline."

"Ease up until you get the facts, missy. Are you heading back to Silverdale now?"

I'm going to check out the rental property Ralph inherited from Norman. I thought maybe if I could see the place firsthand, I could figure out why it was so important to Ralph to get on the property so quickly."

"Be careful. I don't think that guy is anyone to mess with. He might be a killer."

"I'll be careful. I promise. I just want to have a look."

16

The Port Townsend sky had a pink gleam that shone across the calm water. Judy drove slowly through the small, quiet town as dusk fell. She stopped for a moment at a small break in the shops along the main street to enjoy the glow behind the boats along the coast. The sun had completely disappeared by the time she traveled to the north end of town.

Judy stopped her car in front of the cottage next door to the one Ralph now owned. She turned her lights off as she pulled off the road. She put a small notepad in her back pocket and gripped her cell phone in her hand as she got out of her car. Judy wasn't accustomed to carrying a purse. She found it to be a bother. She stood silently on the sidewalk for several minutes, staring at the windows of the quaint bungalow. She didn't hear a sound or see a light anywhere in the tiny dwelling. As she stepped between Ralph's property and the one adjacent to it, she detected a glow of light coming from behind the buildings.

Judy moved between the two properties to see the silhouette of a man in a lawn chair facing the water. Between the gentle tide and the seemingly lifeless man, a fire flickered. Judy moved slowly in the direction of the fire, carefully staying behind the person in the chair. She wanted to approach without being detected. As she moved closer, she stepped from the grass into the damp sand. She could hear the soft pop of the crackling fire along with music playing in the distance. The faint melody seemed to be coming from another bungalow several properties away. With the rear entrances of the row of rentals all backing up to the openness of the surf and sand, it was hard to tell exactly where the source of the music resided.

Judy recognized the stationary man to be Ralph Creech as she crept within steps of the faded lawn chair. His arms hung loosely at his sides. An empty bottle of tequila rested in the sand beneath his right hand. The fire continued to crackle. Judy could feel its warmth against her face. She turned slightly to look at Ralph, but there was no reaction on his part. His eyes were closed. He remained still.

The moon broke through the clouds, heaving a glowing reflection on the water. Judy turned towards the water in amazement of its vastness. Suddenly, she felt something clutch her wrist. It was Ralph's right hand. She tried to pull away from him, but he gripped her arm tightly. She gasped as she looked down at him. He didn't stand. His chin tilted slightly upward until his bloodshot eyes met her shocked stare.

"Let go!" she screamed.

"What are you doing here?" he huffed. "This is private property. You have no business here."

"I wanted to talk to you again. I saw you sitting back here at the fire pit. You were asleep."

"*Passed out* is more like it," he said as he glanced down at the clear glass bottle in the sand.

"Let go of me," she said more softly now, with a stern look, as she continued to try to pull away from his grip.

He let go as she pulled backward, causing her to stumble towards the fire. She caught herself short of the flames and turned back to meet his stare once again. "Why are you here? Why was it so important to you to be here tonight? I understand that you reimbursed the vacation renters and forced them to vacate the property. Why? So that you could sit here and drink yourself into a coma?"

"Something like that. It's none of your business what I'm doing here. This is my property, and I'll do what I like on it."

Judy considered flattering him but quickly decided he may take it the wrong way, which might put her in more danger. There didn't seem to be anyone around to hear her scream. She told her mom that she would be careful. She had already broken that promise by getting close enough to end up in this man's powerful grasp. She studied his face, trying to decide if he could be a murderer. Had he killed his uncle? Might he kill her if she didn't convince him that her visit was harmless? She couldn't be sure of the answers to those questions, but the reporter in her made her ask again, "Why are you here? What is so important about this place that you had to be here tonight?"

"I'm sure I don't seem like a sentimental person, and I'm not. I decided I should show Uncle Norman some respect by attending his funeral. I watched as they lowered him into the ground. Noting the number of mourners, or lack thereof, caused me to reflect on my life. I've done some things I now regret. Things I'm not proud of. I don't have any more friends than old Norman did. I don't even have a kind woman to care for me like he did. I miss Aunt Laura. She was good to both of us. I regret that I didn't stay in touch. Some of the best memories of my life are those that she created for me right here on this beach. I was touched that this is what he left to me. I know it was Aunt Laura's idea, but that makes it all the more meaningful. I was happy and carefree when I was here as a child. I felt loved and cherished. I wanted to feel that again. I came here tonight in search of a memory. Nothing more."

"Ralph." He had gazed out over the vast water as he spoke about his youth, and now Judy paused until she had his attention. "Did you kill Norman?"

"No. No, I didn't. You have your answers. The only answers I'm going to give you. Now run along."

17

━━ ✦ ━━

"**M**r. Proctor, thank you for meeting with me today. Do you mind if I take some notes?" Judy took a small pad from her purse and smiled brightly at the grocery store manager.

"No, not at all. What is this about? You made reference to the police being involved."

"Yes. Do you know Mr. Norman Creech?"

"Yes. He had been a long-time customer of ours. We delivered groceries to his home for most of the past year. I was very sad to hear of his passing."

"Have you heard from Detective Handler?"

"No. I don't know that name. I was contacted by the local police department and the health department about a possible recall on my milk, but they called back to tell me that there was no need to pull my milk or worry about the recall."

"Really? Who contacted you about the milk?"

"I don't know their names, but someone from the police force called originally and told me someone from the health department would likely become involved. As I said, they called back after I pulled all the milk to the back cooler and told me it was safe to restock the shelves. Should I be worried about the milk?"

"No. It sounds like the milk situation has been cleared up. I'm sorry to have wasted your time."

"What does the milk have to do with Mr. Creech?"

"I'm not sure the two turned out to be related. While I'm here, could I speak to the person who normally delivered Mr. Creech's groceries?"

"You are. I usually delivered to Mr. Creech personally. I hate to speak ill of the dead, but he wasn't a very pleasant man. My staff did not appreciate dealing with him. He could be short with my staff and rude to them. He lived near me, so I would take his order to him on my way home in an effort to spare the staff. My employees appreciated not being asked to go to Mr. Creech's house."

"Did *you* find Mr. Creech to be difficult?"

"He wasn't a pleasant man to talk to, but I understand he was not in good health. I imagine it's difficult to have a positive attitude toward others when you are alone and dealing with an ongoing illness on a daily basis. I didn't let his demeanor bother me. I tried to be upbeat and pleasant to him in any event."

"That's very understanding of you. How did you become aware of his illness?"

"Mr. Creech was not apprehensive about telling me about his ailments. He complained about liver disease cheating him out of the rest of his life. I assume that is what he died from. Are you writing a story about Mr. Creech?"

"I may. I'm investigating the possibility of a story. I appreciate you taking the time to talk with me today. I think I have everything I need for now."

Judy left the market and hurried to her car. She flipped back through her notepad until she found Detective Handler's number scribbled on one of the pages. She quickly dialed and put the phone to her ear as she got back into her car.

"Detective Handler. How can I help you?"

"How do you know the milk is okay to drink?" Judy spoke abruptly.

"I'm sorry, who is this?"

"Judy Pine. I just spoke to the manager at the grocery store. How do you know the milk is okay to drink? Why did you tell him he could put it back on the shelf?"

"That isn't any of your business, Miss Pine."

"I'm afraid it is my business. You closed my mom's restaurant down for extensive testing when you thought her cookie killed Norman Creech. Now that you have learned he died from cyanide in the milk, you should be exercising the same precautions with the store where the milk was purchased. My mother will be suing your department for discrimination. You singled her out under different treatment of the law."

"I have done no such thing," Detective Handler responded in an overly confident manner.

"You'll be hearing from our lawyer."

"I imagine you got your information from that little store a couple of miles from Mr. Creech's residence."

"Yes. He told me that you never set foot in his store, and you told him it was okay to put the milk back on the shelf."

"We discovered that the milk did not come from the store near Norman Creech's house."

"Jeff said all of Norman's food came from that store."

"Jeff Donavan later recalled that he brought the milk from his house. He shops at the big retail store closer to his office. We have confirmed that none of the other milk in that store, available the day Jeff bought his milk, was contaminated. As I said, not that it is any of your business. You should leave this case alone, and let the professionals do their jobs."

"I guess that makes Jeff Donavan the prime suspect. He brought the milk that killed his uncle to him and then inherited all his money. Except for the fact that Jeff knew Mr. Creech was dying, and he has pledged almost all of the money to Mrs. Carver's foundation. Had the milk been opened? Had Jeff consumed any of the milk? Maybe someone was trying to kill Jeff."

"I'm sorry, I shouldn't be discussing any of this with you. The point is you don't need to call your lawyer. We did not treat your mother unfairly."

"Understood. Will you please let me know once you have solved this crime? I would like to do a feature story on you, Detective Handler."

"If you will keep your nose out of this case in the meantime, I will be happy to do so."

"Thank you, Detective Handler." Judy hung up the phone. She did not intend to keep her nose out of the case, but she did intend to write a story. It would feature the truth, which may or may not feature Detective Handler in a positive manner.

18

Lily was checking on customers in the dining room when Ken Valentine walked into the restaurant. She finished her conversation at a table while she watched the hostess seat Ken at a small booth on the far wall of the dining room.

Lily smiled brightly as she approached Ken's table. "Hi, Ken. Nice to see you."

"I'm sorry I haven't been in for a while. I'm also sorry that I didn't make good on the lunch date with our daughters the other day. You know how I hate to get out in the rain. The dampness plays havoc with my arthritis. I came by today to offer an official apology."

"Apology accepted. I'm glad to see you. I'm surprised to see you out and about without Renee."

"She's over in Seattle today. Something about lingerie modeling. I don't plan on seeing her for the rest of the day. Her day likely includes cocktails and men and will run late into the evening. I try not to think about it. The girl is a grown adult, but she still acts like a wild teenager most of the time. No point in growing up too quickly, I guess." Ken shrugged.

"She certainly has a wild spirit all her own. She told me she was once arrested for dancing in the town fountain in her bra and panties." Lily laughed.

"The nice policeman escorted her out of the fountain and into a blanket before driving her home. She didn't actually get arrested. Maybe she should have. She gets away with quite a bit of mischief around town. Everyone knows her and finds her to be amusing and eccentric. I suppose she never harms anyone. She's just having fun."

"Always," Lily said with a wide smile and an agreeing nod.

"I noticed you at Noman Creech's funeral the other day. I didn't know you knew Norm. It's hard to believe he managed to make a new friend in the past year. The man has been a recluse since his wife died. Most people preferred that he kept to himself."

"It's more of a friend of a friend... or a friend of a friend of a relative kind of relationship."

"Twice removed on his wife's side I bet." Ken laughed.

"Yes. That's about right. Judy and I were just paying our respects. I'm sorry we didn't get a chance to say hello. When you left, it didn't seem polite to speak. We stayed until the ceremony had concluded."

"I was there out of respect for the family and... well... because I wanted to be sure he was really dead. I know that sounds awful, but I wanted to watch them lower that old geezer into the ground. I didn't want to stick around to hear anyone say any kind words over him."

"Why did you dislike him? You must have had quite a past with him."

"Norm and I were friends and business partners at one time. We met at a time when we were both starting to build our businesses. We had invested in several properties together over the years. We dined together with our wives and spent time fishing and playing golf together. All the good friend things. You know. Just having fun like Renee does."

"What changed? Why do you dislike him so much now?" Lily decided not to let on that Renee had already given an overview of the feud between the two men.

"We decided to partner on a large property venture a while back. I had an inside track on some land that would surely be worth millions down the road. I was tight on capital at the time due to some other investments I had made. Norm agreed to financially back me in the deal for a percentage. When it came time to close the deal, Norm closed it without me. He made a small fortune on the land and left me out in the cold. I haven't spoken to him since."

"I guess it's hard to say what some people will do when there's a pile of money at stake. Greed can overcome friendship for some."

"Not for me. I would have given that guy my last dollar if he needed it. Up until the moment he screwed me out of that deal, I thought we were best friends. I loved him like a brother."

"I'm sorry about that." Lily didn't know what to say. She was saddened by the telling of the story.

"Let's not dwell on that old coot. Join me for a drink in honor of my delightful yet childish daughter." He smiled brightly and Lily couldn't refuse. She took a seat across from Ken Valentine and waved for the waitress.

19

Judy drove to Jeff Donavan's office. Mrs. Brown wasn't at the reception desk, so Judy walked down the hall to Jeff's office. "Hey, Jeff. How's it going?"

"I'm doing as well as can be expected under the circumstances. What can I do for you?" Jeff said with a quizzical look.

"Detective Handler told me that the milk your uncle drank was delivered by you, from your house."

"That's true. I had forgotten that I called Uncle Norman on my way to his house. If you recall, I stopped at my house for some paperwork. Uncle Norman demanded that I bring him some milk if I was going to bring a lunch containing a cookie. It seems he was out of milk. I didn't have time to go to the store, but I had just purchased milk the day before. I took the unopened carton of milk from my house to Norman, along with the box lunch from the charity luncheon that Mrs. Carver had given me. When I got to his house, I helped him to the table, opened the box, and poured him a glass of milk. I left him at the table and went back to work."

"Do you think someone intended that you drink the milk? Maybe you were the target. Your uncle may have been killed inadvertently by someone who was trying to kill you." Judy's eyes opened wide with the thought.

"I don't see any reason why anyone would want to kill me. That's ridiculous. I apologize for cutting this short, but I have an appointment with a client. I really must go."

"I know I barged in here unannounced, but don't you think a possible attempt on your life might need to take precedent over your client appointment?"

"Mr. Donavan," Mrs. Brown called from the hallway. "So sorry. I didn't know you were with someone." She stopped in the office doorway. "It's just that you are going to be late."

"I was just telling Miss Pine that very thing. Please show Miss Pine out. Thank you, Mrs. Brown." Jeff picked up his briefcase and nodded at the ladies as he hurried down the hall.

Judy paused, rubbing her chin softly with her index finger.

"Will there be something else?" Mrs. Brown asked, noticing that Judy did not seem to be on her way out.

"He seems quite happy today in spite of finding out there may have been a threat on his life."

"Mr. Donavan is almost always happy. He has a very positive outlook on life. He is quite refreshing to be around."

"I bet that's a great type of person to work with."

"Oh, yes. He has been a terrific addition to the office here. He cheers everyone up with his can-do attitude and his sunshiny disposition."

"I like to think that I have a positive outlook, but I don't feel especially jubilant every day," Judy smirked.

"I know what you mean. Some days I walk in here feeling like I just want to go back to bed. His attitude can be contagious. I find, more often than not, that his smiling face helps me start my day on a positive note. I only remember him being melancholy during one period of his time here. That was when his poor aunt died in that terrible accident."

"Someone mentioned the accident to me before. It may have been you. That was sometime in the past year, as I remember."

"Yes. It was about eight months ago, I think. Horrible. I'm glad I wasn't there to witness the accident. Her car was reported to be completely totaled. She died at the scene. She was a wonderful person. She was nothing like her husband. She deserved better than to be with him."

"It must have been a horrendous crash. Was there another vehicle involved? Was anyone else hurt?"

"I think the report said her car was hit on the driver's side by a semi. The driver didn't stop. He kept on going."

"A hit-and-run? Did they find the truck driver?"

"Not that I know of. Mr. Donavan always said it didn't matter. Finding the driver wouldn't bring her back. After a few days, he was back to his old self again."

"That is a terrible way to dieJudy squinted her eyes, trying to erase the image that came into her head.

"It was all over the news for a while. They were looking for a big red truck of some type. I forget the make and model. They had witnesses, but I don't know that the driver was ever arrested."

"I've taken up enough of your time, Mrs. Brown. I can see myself out."

Mrs. Brown stepped back into the hallway and stood to one side to let Judy pass.

20

— · —

Brick and Nellie led Judy and Lily along the wood decking near the bay. The wind was cool and dry, but the sun shone from a bright blue sky. The ladies wore sweaters, but the hairy canines with them were unphased by the cool breeze.

"So, Ken Valentine told you he was happy Norman Creech was dead, and he only showed up at the funeral to make sure he was buried?" Judy scoffed.

"Not in those exact words but pretty much, yes," Lily responded. "He didn't admit to killing him... just wanting him to be dead. He made no qualms about the fact that he no longer liked Mr. Creech. They had been close friends until the day Norman cheated Ken out of the property deal. Ken says he never talked to him again after that. It would be awfully odd for him to admit these feelings to anyone if he had killed Mr. Creech. Don't you think?"

"The staff at Donavan's office all had similar feelings about Mr. Creech. They all had stories about how badly

Norman treated Jeff. Mrs. Brown was just as forthcoming with her contempt for Norman."

Lily's phone rang. She pulled it from her pocket to look at the caller ID.

"It's Doug."

"Oh, good. Let's see what he knows."

"Hey, Doug. How are you feeling?" Lily asked.

"I'm feeling much better. I'm getting along okay on the crutches. Later today, I'm going to talk with my boss about getting back to work," Doug said.

"Oh, good. I think your pal Handler needs some help," Judy blurted out.

"By the way, I have Judy here with me," Lily said with a grin only Judy could see.

"Did you hear about the milk that killed Mr. Creech?" Judy went on. "It came from Jeff Donavan's house. Jeff claims it did anyway. Handler was pretty smug when I talked to him. He didn't offer much in the way of details, but he didn't seem to have many questions about how the milk became tainted. From the sound of his voice, it seemed like he didn't have a care in the world."

"He thinks he has the case all wrapped up," Doug said. "He found a syringe and a cyanide vile in Ralph Creech's F150. He is prosecuting him for the attempted murder of Jeff Donavan and the murder of his uncle, Norman Creech. He had several million motives for the murder of Jeff Donavan, knowing his uncle was going to die soon."

"I suppose, even if he didn't know what was in the will, he could assume that he would at least be sharing the wealth with Jeff," Lily said. "He told us he spoke with his uncle a few weeks before he died. Norman may have told Ralph about the will."

"I guess Handler stopped worrying about the milk once he was sure he knew who poisoned it," Judy was stewing. "So, his theory is that Ralph poisoned the milk in Jeff's house in an attempt to kill him. Norman insisted that Jeff buy him some milk, and Jeff took the poisoned milk from his refrigerator, without knowing it was poisoned, to Norman."

"That pretty much sums it up," Doug responded.

"I wonder if Detective Handler will give me an exclusive on this case. Do you think he'll let me talk to Ralph Creech?" Judy asked Doug.

"I doubt it. I think you've somehow rubbed him the wrong way. It would be best for all of us if you don't let on that you know all of this. I probably shouldn't have told you." Doug hoped Judy would keep this to herself for now.

"I'll try to get Handler to meet with me as a follow-up." Judy wanted to relieve Doug of his concerns. "I'll play to his ego. He seems like the kind of guy who would like me to publish a story about how smart he is and how his brilliance closed the case. Don't worry, I'll keep you out of it."

"Thank you for that," Doug replied.

"The best part is that the restaurant is totally out of the story," Lily said happily. "My food had nothing to do with any of this. Ralph and the milk killed that poor man. Not my cookie."

"I won't even mention your cookies in the story," Judy assured her. "Doug, didn't you say you were hit by a hit-and-run driver in a semitruck?"

"Yes. Officer Crum is working on the case. I should say *Detective* Crum. He just made detective. This is his first official case as a detective. I think he may have a lead on the company the truck came from. He got a good tip from one of the eyewitnesses to the accident. Why do you ask? Are you starting your next story?"

"Interesting coincidence," Judy said. "I was talking with Mrs. Brown yesterday, and she told me that Laura Creech, Jeff Donavan's aunt, was killed by a hit-and-run driver... in a large semi."

"Unfortunate coincidence," Lily added.

"I normally don't believe in coincidences, but I don't know how the two incidences could be related," Doug said. "I'll be sure to mention it to Crum just in case it can be helpful. I need to get off the phone. I'm due to have that call with my lieutenant."

"Okay. Good luck," Lily said as she hung up her cell phone.

21

Judy walked into the interrogation room with Ralph Creech's lawyer. They hadn't spoken since they entered the hallway at the prison. Ralph agreed to meet with Judy, but his lawyer thought it was a bad idea. He made no attempt to keep that fact a secret. Ralph was already seated in the drab grey room when Judy stepped through the doorway. The lawyer nodded at Ralph, and Ralph, in turn, gave him a thumbs up. The lawyer left the room, and Judy heard the door lock behind her. A guard stood along the wall next to the door. He glanced at Judy and then fixed his eyes back on Ralph without saying a word. He wouldn't be participating in the interview.

"Hi Ralph," Judy started the conversation as she slid the metal folding chair back from the table to take a seat.

"I hope you can forgive my manners if I don't get up," Ralph said, looking down at his cuffs that were anchored to the heavy metal table between them. He kept his eyes low, looking dejected.

"You injected cyanide into Jeff Donavan's milk in an attempt to kill him." Judy opened her notepad. "You killed your uncle instead. Jeff inherited everything. Almost everything. Very ironic, wouldn't you say?"

"Very trumped up. I would say. I didn't do any of this. I've been framed."

"Come now. I've heard this song and dance a thousand times. If you think I'm going to print lies on the word of an alleged killer, you are barking up the wrong tree. How about you tell me what really happened? I'd like to tell the story of Norman and Laura Creech from the eyes of their nephew."

"Uncle Norman was dying. I learned that from him the day he called me. I told you and your mom about the call. While we were talking, he got pretty emotional about missing Laura. He was sobbing on the phone like I'd never heard a man do before. As we took a trip down memory lane together, Norman remembered that he hadn't updated his will. He told me he was sure it still listed Jeff as his sole benefactor. He and Aunt Laura had their trust set to go to him in the case of their deaths. He only agreed to that to please Laura. Uncle Norman said he would get that all changed. He would reassign the trust to me. He didn't want Jeff to get any of it."

"Do you remember talking with me at the beach?"

"I do. It's a bit fuzzy, but I remember."

"You didn't say anything about the will then."

"I didn't think it was any of your business. It still isn't, but I didn't know who else to talk to. I doubt anyone is going to believe me."

"You told me the property on the water was an important part of your childhood."

"I loved to go there when I was a kid. Several years ago, Laura told me she wanted me to have it. Norman wouldn't agree to give it to me at that time. He refused to stop renting it out to tourists. He acted like he needed the money. The compromise was that I would get it once he died. Until I received the notice about the will, I didn't know for sure if I would get it." Ralph's sorrowful face turned into a cheerful grin. "Aunt Laura had a way of dealing with Uncle Norman. She could handle him like no one else could."

"Can you tell me about Laura's death?"

"I know as much as you can read in the papers. She was hit at an intersection by a large truck. She died in the street from her injuries. The driver drove off. To my knowledge, they never found the driver responsible for the accident. Norman kept to himself entirely after that."

"I can corroborate all of this. I'll follow up on your story about the will and about the syringe being planted. You allowed me access to your file. I read every bit of it. Detective Handler found the syringe and the vile while serving a warrant for your property. I understand he also found a witness that will testify that you were in town near

Jeff Donavan's place on the morning of the murder. Even if Norman intended to change the will, he didn't. All the evidence points to you being the killer."

"I guess I don't have anything else to say to you, Miss Pine. You can go."

"Would you like to talk about why you needed the money? You could tell me more about your memories of kayaking with your uncle. Tell me how your aunt and uncle met. Things like that."

"No. We are done. You can leave now." Ralph's face started to turn red. Judy could see a large vein growing on his forehead. He started to clench his fists tightly in front of him.

"Okay. I'm leaving. If you change your mind. If you want to talk on or off the record, have your lawyer get in touch with me." Judy stood and backed up towards the door. The guard rapped on the door, and Judy heard the lock click.

Ralph's lawyer escorted Judy back to the entrance to the courthouse and stepped outside with her. He stopped on the steps and said, "Unless he takes a plea deal, this is going to trial. I'd appreciate it if you didn't print a story about him until after the trial."

"Can you defend him at trial? Can you bring reasonable doubt with all the hard evidence the prosecutor has? Does he have a chance at being found innocent?"

"I'm still looking into it, but currently, I'm recommending he take a plea deal if one is offered. The prosecutor can show motive, opportunity, and evidence of the murder weapon. Ralph has some skeletons in his closet that won't bode well for his character. I'm at a loss for how to help him out here."

"Do you think he did it? Do you think he killed his uncle?"

"I have no idea. It doesn't matter what I think. My job is to defend him to the best of my ability."

"I believe him. I believe he's innocent. I'm not sure why, but I do. I'll do what I can to help you. Maybe a well-written story about a kinder, gentler Ralph Creech would be of some help."

22

"Hi ladies. I'm Detective Peter Crum. Thank you for meeting with me," Detective Crum said as he took a seat next to Lily and Judy in the dining room at Marty's on the Bay.

"Detective, it's nice to meet you. We've heard good things about you from Doug Miller," Lily smiled.

Judy already had a notepad lying on the table. "You don't mind if I take some notes too, do you?" She nodded a greeting.

"Not at all. Detective Miller told me you were a reporter," he replied with a friendly smile.

"You said this was about Doug Miller's hit-and-run," Lily said. "I don't know how we can help you. We weren't there when it happened. We first heard about it a few hours later from a friend here in town."

"I'm here about a tip you gave us," Detective Crum looked directly at Judy as he spoke.

"Did I give you a tip?" Judy asked.

"You told Detective Miller about another hit-and-run. Different but similar. It was a long shot that they would have any connection whatsoever. You understand, there are hundreds of hit-and-runs, every day, and the likelihood of any two that happen months apart would be related... well, it's unheard of. I wasn't having much luck, so I decided to look into Laura Creech's hit-and-run case. I got all of the records from the Port Townsend Police Department. I'm not sure how they didn't close that case at the time. I was able to follow the evidence to a truck belonging to a trucking company that is owned by Leon Hays. His sister is Jeff Donavan's secretary."

"Kathryn Brown? The truck that was involved belonged to her brother?" Judy asked.

"Yes." Detective Crum raised his eyes with approval.

"So, someone who worked for Kathryn Brown's brother ran Laura Creech down and then fled the scene?" Lily concluded.

"Not someone who worked for him- Mr. Hays," the detective said. "The truck logs show that he was driving the truck at the time Mrs. Creech was killed. The logs also show that Leon Hays was driving the truck at the time Detective Miller was hit on the Narrows Bridge. I was able to get trace from the truck that matches Detective Miller's car. The case against Leon Hays in the Laura Creech case is more circumstantial, but it led me to the truck that surely hit Detective Miller."

"Wow. What are the odds?" Judy shared her amazement. "Mrs. Brown hated Norman Creech. She didn't think much of Ralph either. Maybe she had her brother kill Laura and Norman to get money for her boss and friend, Jeff Donavan, and then framed Ralph Creech."

"But why have her brother run into Doug?" Lily was confused.

"Maybe she knows Doug and Detective Handler, at least by reputation, and she assumed her odds of getting away with the murder were better if Handler was running the investigation," Judy went on.

"I did come here hoping you two could help me tie the two hit-and-runs together to help with the older case. I think this theory sounds like a bit of a stretch." The detective jotted some notes on a small pad and paused for a moment, clicking his pen. "If you're right, I could blow the lid off a murder investigation. That would be a pretty big collar for a new detective." He grinned at the ladies.

"I interviewed Ralph Creech. He claims innocence. He maintains his uncle was about to change his will, leaving Jeff Donavan out of it entirely. Mrs. Brown could have found out about it."

"Maybe I can get her to come down to the station for a talk. I don't have anything to arrest her on, but with her brother behind bars, she might come in willingly to try to help him," Detective Crum said. "I can lay out the circumstantial evidence and see if I can get her to come clean. If she did it, that is."

23

"Hey, Mom. Are you home?" Judy asked as she let herself in the front door of her mother's condo.

"Come on in. Jed and I were about to have dinner," Lily responded. "Would you like some?"

Nellie and Brick met Judy at the door. She scratched each of the dogs on the head and told them they were good dogs. They were very familiar with Judy and didn't bark as she entered. Nellie dropped to the floor and rolled to her back for a quick belly rub.

"Hi Jed," Judy said as she joined Lily and Jed at the kitchen table. "I ate earlier, but what are you having?"

"We both had late days at work, so we decided to wait for dinner," Lily said.

"I call it 'Chicken Lily'. It's one of my favorite dishes. Baked chicken with mushrooms, onions, and cheese, covered in cream sauce," Jed said.

"I love that dish! I'll eat again if you have enough." Judy exclaimed.

"Oh, yes. There's plenty. We have rice and broccoli to go with the chicken," Lily responded.

"Cream sauce on everything for me, please." Jed's eyes widened as Lily filled a plate covering everything with a generous portion of white cream pepper sauce.

"I talked to Detective Crum on the way here. He brought Kathryn Brown in for questioning. He made sure Leon saw her there."

"I suppose Leon could have met Mr. Donavan through Kathryn," Judy commented.

"He said Jeff Donavan does his books for the transportation company," Judy went on. "They likely worked closely on the company profit and loss statements. Peter told me that his preliminary investigation showed that Mr. Hays's trucking business was deep in the red. Peter also said he would try to substantiate the claim that the two men worked on the books together."

"Is it *Peter* now?" Lily grinned at her daughter.

"Yes, Detective Crum told me I could call him Peter," Judy said without giving her mother the benefit of a reaction.

"If this Donavan character knew the trucking guy needed money, he might have approached him with a deal. Desperate times and all of that," Jed said as he took another bite of his white cream sauce-covered chicken. "You've really outdone yourself, Lily."

"Peter is hoping to get more information out of Leon. More to come for sure. I'm going to work on some of the leads with Peter... Detective Crum... tomorrow. This is delicious, Mom."

"Thank you both," Lily said as she sipped from her wine glass. "What about the evidence found in Ralph Creech's truck? How does this all lead to him? It seems they have motive, opportunity, and evidence of the murder weapon on Ralph. What do the two truck accidents- or should we say assaults- have to do with Ralph?"

"I'm not sure about that yet. Like I said... more to come," Judy said. "You know what Doug would say.

"Follow the evidence," Lily said with a laugh.

24

"Hi, Jeff. Do you mind if I ask you a few questions for my story?" Judy asked from Jeff Donavan's front door. "I talked to Ralph yesterday. It looks like he's on the hook for murder and attempted murder."

"Yes, I know. What can I tell you that you don't already know? This is a terrible murder that should not be sensationalized. He tried to kill me and, in turn, cost my uncle several months of his life."

"I agree. This is all a horrible injustice. I'd like to tell the public about the good that came of it. I understand you were able to claim your inheritance, and you are planning to donate most of it to cancer research through Mrs. Carver's charity organization. I was hoping to talk to you about why this particular charity is so near and dear to your heart. The feel-good part of the story."

"I don't have time right now. Call my office. I'll make sure Mrs. Brown schedules time for us to talk."

"Are you sure? It will only take a few minutes. I just need a few details for the article. I'll be happy to run it by you before I publish it."

"I don't have time right now. Call my office, and I'll be happy to talk to you later."

"Okay. I'll call Mrs. Brown. You heard about her brother, I assume."

"What about him?"

Judy could tell she had Jeff's full attention now. "He has been arrested for a hit-and-run. Will Mrs. Brown be at the office today if I call?"

"I'm sorry, Miss Pine. I really must go." He closed the door between them.

Judy walked across the street and slid behind the wheel of her BMW. Her phone rang as she started the car.

"Judy. This is Doug. When Leon found out his sister may be prosecuted, he confessed to both of the hit-and-runs. He's working on a plea deal. He has implicated Jeff Donavan in both Laura's murder and my assault. He claims Jeff paid him to kill his aunt and then to make sure I was off the case when his uncle died."

"Holy crap, Doug!" Judy had started to drive away from Jeff's house but stopped the car along the curb, stunned by what Doug was saying. She glanced in her rearview mirror and saw Jeff Donavan crossing the street with a large suitcase and a duffle bag. He loaded the luggage into his trunk and hurried to the driver's seat. Judy ducked down as Jeff drove past her.

"Judy? Judy? Are you still there?" came over her car speaker.

"Yes. I was trying to get some information out of Jeff Donavan. I'm outside his house right now. He just loaded two bags into his car and took off. I'm going to follow him."

"That's probably not a good idea, Judy."

"I'm sure you're right, but I'm doing it anyway. I bet he's heading to the airport. He has no intentions of giving any of that money to charity."

"Crum is getting a warrant as we speak. I'll send some patrol cars to pick him up. You keep your distance."

Judy followed Jeff for almost an hour. She saw no sign of any police cars along the way. If he was going to Sea-Tac airport, he wasn't taking the shortest route. He pulled into an upscale neighborhood and slowed to a stop in front of a large saltbox house. Judy stopped about fifty yards behind him and ducked down in her car again. She sent Doug her location. Her phone rang.

"Doug! Where are the cops?" Judy yelled at the car speaker after clicking the call button on her steering wheel. "He stopped at the location I sent you, but I don't know how long we'll be here."

"They should have had him by now. I'm unsure what happened, but my APB was called off. I have issued another one. Just to be safe, I called one of the officers in the area on his personal cell. He'll be able to get to your location quickly."

"Here he comes. He's getting back in his car. I'm going to stay on him."

"You should let the police handle it from here. Stay where you are until I tell you he's been apprehended."

"He could get away. This isn't my first time tailing someone. I'll hang back. He won't know I'm watching him. I'll just keep track of him until I see blue lights flashing."

Doug stayed on the line with Judy as she followed Jeff Donavan back to the highway. They traveled only a few miles before he took another exit. "He's getting off the highway again. We are heading into Bremerton," she told Doug. "Good thing I stayed with him. He might have disappeared altogether."

"Don't get too close," he warned her.

"He's pulling down Rocky Point Road. We are headed down the bay road. He turned off, to the left, into one of the driveways. I drove past him. I'm going to pull into one of the driveways a few houses away and watch to make sure he doesn't leave. Get on the horn and get the police over here."

"I'm on it. Keep the line open. I'll be right back with you."

Judy backed into a driveway three houses away from where Jeff pulled off the road. The house at the end of the driveway looked deserted. She watched intently through her passenger-side window. She wasn't about to let him get away without her knowing. She was starting to get anxious. She could feel the sweat drip off her forehead as she tapped her fingers nervously on the edge of the passenger seat.

There was a hard bang on the BMW's driver's side window, and the glass shattered into Judy's lap. She screamed as Jeff unlocked the door and swung it open in one motion. He grabbed Judy by the arm and pulled her from the small coupe. She heard Doug's voice on her car speaker as she was flung from the car.

"Why are you following me? What do you know?" He yelled as he forced her to the ground.

"I'm a reporter. I'm just trying to get a story." She stayed on the ground looking up at him. She wanted to stay within earshot of the car. She hoped Doug could hear what was going on.

"I know the cops are onto me. They have a warrant out for my arrest. I bet you and your mom are to blame for this."

"She didn't know how Jeff knew there was an APB out for his arrest, but she thought convincing him that it wasn't for suspicion of murder would work in her favor. "Leon Hays," she said softly.

"What about Leon? I'm his accountant. So what?"

"He has been arrested for a hit-and-run. He ran someone off the road and fled the scene."

"What does that have to do with me? That doesn't explain why the police are after me."

"Leon Hays implicated you. He said you paid him to run the guy off the road."

"What else? What else are the cops after me for?"

"Nothing that I know of. I got a tip about the hit-and-run. Since I knew you from your uncle's case, I wanted to scoop the story. I was going to blindside you with questions about Leon after I got you talking about your good work with the charity. Since you wouldn't talk to me, I decided to follow you when I saw you leaving your house. Investigative reporting."

"You are ruining everything. Get up. Walk up the drive." He pointed towards the still house. As they crossed a small patio at the front of the dark home, he tapped one of the rusted, dirty chairs that rested on the mossy patio. "Sit down. I have to figure out what to do."

"It's your word against his. You should turn yourself in and make your case. Just because Leon says you paid him to commit vehicular assault, doesn't mean he can prove it." Judy hoped to calm him. She didn't want him doing anything hasty.

"No. I have to get out of here. I'm not going to jail."

"I know you don't want to add kidnapping to the charges against you. You should let me go. If you leave now, you can likely get away. If you do get caught, all they have on you is a witness account from a man who is being held for attempted assault."

"Kidnapping? I didn't kidnap you. You followed me here!" he leaned down and began to scream into her face.

"I didn't say you kidnapped me. I said you don't want to go that far. That's all I'm saying. Don't give the cops more fuel." Her attempt to calm him wasn't working.

Judy could hear sirens in the distance. They were getting closer. As the sound of the police cars grew nearer, Jeff turned and ran back towards the driveway he had pulled his car into. Within seconds, a city police car screeched to a halt in front of Judy's car. "He's over there." Judy pointed in the direction Jeff had run as two police officers exited the vehicle with their sidearms drawn.

"Are you okay? Is there anyone here with you?" one of the officers said as he converged on Judy.

"I'm okay. He's trying to get away," she said as she moved towards the road. She looked in the direction she had been surveilling earlier from her car. Two police cruisers sat at the end of the driveway. A uniformed officer steered Jeff to the back seat of one of the cars. Jeff Donavan's hands were cuffed behind his back.

25

J udy walked back to her car after spending almost an hour debriefing with the officers on the scene. She pulled her car door opened and listened to the tiny pieces of glass shift inside her vehicle. She grabbed a jacket from the back seat and used it to cautiously rake the safety glass from the driver's seat. She sat behind the wheel and started her car. She paused briefly and let out a heavy sigh.

"Judy. Are you okay?" Doug said over the car speakers.

Judy jumped at the sound of his voice. "I am. Except you almost gave me a heart attack just now. The cavalry showed up in the nick of time. I'm surprised that you're still on the line. It must be over an hour by now."

"I've been in touch with one of the officers onsite, but I wanted to hear from you that everything was okay."

"I'm fine. I'm just a bit jittery, I guess. I wasn't sure what that guy might do to me. He may think he's just being arrested for suspicion of paying for an assault."

"On top of two murder charges."

"I don't know if he knows, but we know that."

"He'll know soon enough. Leon Hays can prove he was paid for the attacks. He even has a voice recording of Jeff from when he agreed to pay to have his aunt killed. He said he was keeping it for insurance."

"I understand why he killed his aunt. He wanted the money. Once he found out Norman was dying, she was the only thing standing between Mr. Donavan and his fortune."

"But then, he found out old Mr. Creech was going to change his will, leaving everything to Cousin Ralph. He couldn't let that happen. So, he hurried Norman's death along with the tainted milk."

"Why go after you? What did he have to gain from your death?"

"Lily has that part all figured out. I'll let her tell you. You should call her. She's worried about you."

"I'm on it. Thanks, Doug."

26

Judy, Lily, and Doug sat at a large table in the dining room of Lily's restaurant. Chase emptied a large tray of food onto the table. A bucket of beers on ice sat in the center.

Detective Crum neared the table, shaking his head gently from side to side. "Are you sure he's going to show up?"

"He'll show up. He has no idea that he's about to be arrested," Doug assured the young detective.

"He had to consider that Jeff might turn him in," Lily supported Crum's theory.

"Nope. I'm with Doug. He's not a bright guy," Judy laughed as she spoke and pointed towards the door.

Detective Handler walked towards the table, and Detective Crum pulled his handcuffs from behind his back. "You have the right to remain silent..." Detective Crum continued reciting the Miranda rights to Handler as he steered him out of the building.

"They got Donavan to admit he paid Handler off. Just like you thought, Lily." Doug gave Lily an approving smile.

"That sorry excuse for a detective had no idea that Jeff Donavan gave him up to the authorities. I can't believe Jeff had you run over by a truck to get Handler put in charge of the investigation," Lily said.

"That's what you get for being honest and smart," Judy said with a chuckle.

"Jeff got his money's worth with Handler. He kept the investigation pointed in every direction except for Jeff Donavan's. When all else failed, Handler planted evidence in Ralph Creech's truck. That not only solved the murder but also kept Ralph from contesting the will. Handler was able to call off the APB on Donavan, temporarily, but because you were following him, it wasn't long enough for him to escape. I don't think this was Handler's first-time coloring outside the lines. That was his house Jeff stopped at on his way to Bremerton," Doug said.

"That is a pretty fancy house Handler lives in. Much nicer than your place," Judy laughed at Doug.

"That's for sure. You can't afford a place like that on a detective's salary." Doug pulled a beer from the bucket of ice.

RECIPES

Chicken Lily

As a previous restaurant manager and consultant, I love to cook. My humble beginnings in the restaurant business were stationed in a full-service restaurant kitchen. I cook for my wife most evenings. For better or for worse, I like to try new recipe ideas and tweak them over time.

This dish is a variation of a dish once eaten at a Columbus, Ohio restaurant. It's rich, creamy, and cheesy.

Ingredients:

4 chicken breasts

1 large onion diced to ¼ inch

2 cups sliced fresh mushrooms

4 slices of cheddar cheese

2 Tablespoons flour

4 Tablespoons butter

1 oz. Extra Virgin Olive Oil

Salt – to taste

Pepper – to taste

3/4 cup chicken broth

1/2 cup heavy cream

2 cups white rice

3 cups broccoli florets

3 oz. Parmesan cheese

Preheat oven to 375 degrees.

Make rice per directions. I like to use a rice steamer.

Melt 2 tablespoons of butter in a large nonstick skillet.

Add mushrooms and diced onions to the skillet. Sauté on medium heat until soft.

Add 1 oz of Parmesan cheese to the onions and mushrooms. Cook until the cheese is melted.

Lightly oil the bottom of an oven-safe pan.

Lay chicken breasts smooth side down in the pan.

Add a slice of cheese to the center of each chicken breast.

Pour the onion and mushroom mixture over the chicken breasts, topping each evenly.

Roll each breast, placing seam-side down in the pan.

Bake in preheated oven until chicken's internal temperature is 165 degrees.

During the last ten to fifteen minutes of baking time (when the internal temperature of the chicken is at about 150 degrees), start the next steps.

Steam broccoli in salted water until slightly tender.

While broccoli steams, melt 2 tablespoons of butter in a large nonstick skillet under medium heat.

Slowly add chicken broth and then heavy cream, stirring constantly.

Add salt and pepper to taste.

Once the liquid is warm and slightly creamy, add the other 2 ounces of Parmesan cheese. Stir until melted. Reduce heat to low.

Drain Broccoli.

Once the chicken is fully cooked, plate chicken with sides of rice and broccoli.

Top with the cream sauce.

I'm with Jed. I like to put a layer of savory sauce over everything, smothering the rice, broccoli, and chicken.

Killer Broccoli Salad

This is a simple recipe that you can take to any picnic, BBQ, or family gathering. Your friends, family, and neighbors will ask for it time and time again.

Ingredients:

1 large head of broccoli, chopped

1 medium red onion, diced to ¼ inch

1/2 cup pecans, chopped

1/2 cup golden raisins

1 cup mayonnaise

1/4 cup sugar

1 teaspoon cider vinegar

1/4 cup bacon bits

In a large bowl, combine the first four ingredients.

To make the dressing, mix mayonnaise, sugar, and vinegar in a small bowl.

Mix dressing into the broccoli and onion mixture.

Add bacon bits.

Chill before serving.

Death on Bainbridge Island
A Pacific Northwest Cozy Culinary
Book 3 – sample chapter

Chapter 1

Brick sat at attention, looking out the window as rain
ran down the glass pane. The apricot-colored, curly-haired
Goldendoodle was fixated on Judy walking towards her
mother's condo with something tucked under her raincoat. As the knob on the front door turned, Nellie started
to bark while staying a good ten feet from the door. Brick
moved to the edge of the entrance and stood in anticipation of the visitor. His body wagged with eagerness. The
short, stout Petit Basset Griffon Vendéen stopped her bark
and copied Brick's body wag as Judy entered. Judy crossed
the threshold, pulling a small black and tan Yorkshire Terrier from under her pastel blue raincoat. She knelt, letting

the other dogs sniff the small black dog. "This is Jack," Judy said to the two larger dogs. "He's our new family member. You two be nice to Jack." Jack's eyes widened for a few seconds, but after some initial sniffing, the dogs all seemed to relax, and Judy placed the puppy on the floor. There was running and jumping and quite a bit of barking, mostly by the puppy. Nellie seemed cautiously interested, and Brick refused to get into full-play mode. That was probably for the best since the forty-pound, curly-haired dog towered over the two-pound pup.

"Oh, good. You finally brought Jack over for a visit," Lily said as she came from the back of the home. "I know you were worried about Nellie since she's a little sensitive, but Brick is very well-mannered around other dogs. I'm sure they will all get along just fine."

"How long will Brick be staying with you?" Judy asked as she shed her raincoat, leaving it on the doorknob to drip on the entry tile.

"Just a couple of days. Jed is at a food expo. He should be back late tomorrow. He's very lovable and well-mannered." Lily smiled at the large dog.

"Are you talking about Brick or Jed," Judy said with a laugh.

"True of both, I guess, but I was referring to the dog."

"Why do you look like you're dressed for work?"

"I have to go to the restaurant. I'm sorry. I know we planned to spend the morning together, but Chase didn't show up for work this morning. Linda just called a few minutes ago. I need to help them get opened, and I'll stay through lunch if he doesn't show up."

"I'll hang out here with the dogs in case you can come back. They could use the chance to get to know one another. I have some work to do. I'll grab my laptop from the car."

"What are you working on?"

"Ferry boat scheduling changes are on the horizon. The big story," she chuckled. "I have a piece on travel to Canada due after that. I think I have a new angle on it. I'm working on both stories right now. I should have the scheduling piece finished pretty quickly. What's the story with Chase? He's usually pretty reliable, isn't he?"

"Yes. Very."

Chase Raker was the front-of-house manager at Lily's restaurant along Liberty Bay in Poulsbo. He had been with her since she opened last year. Lily relied on him and Linda Holt to hold everything together at the restaurant when she wasn't there and sometimes when she was.

"Doesn't he date that nice girl over at Virgil's café?" Judy asked.

"Yes. Her name is Annie Beazley. I'll check with her to see if she's heard from him. Good idea. The wonderful mind of an investigative reporter," Lily said with a chortle.

"I'll grab my laptop quickly before you leave. Keep an eye on Jack."

"Will do. He sure is an adorable little guy."

"He certainly is. Just like you two," Judy said as she scratched the chins of the other two dogs.

Lily's phone rang as Judy left the condo. She accepted a collect call from the Bainbridge Island Sherriff's department and spoke briefly to someone on the other end. She hung up the phone as Judy reentered the house.

"What's wrong, Mom?" Judy asked. "You have an unsettled look on your face."

"I just talked to Chase. He's in jail at the Bainbridge Police Station. He's not sure when he'll be able to get out."

"What's the charge?"

"Murder."

Please go to **dshock.net** for more books by this Author.

Made in the USA
Columbia, SC
17 July 2023

20142385R00072